MW00899746

DEADLY GOODBYE

A WITCH IN THE WOODS

JENNA ST. JAMES

Deadly Goodbye

Jenna St. James

Copyright © 2022 by Jenna St. James.

Published by Jenna St. James

All Rights Reserved. No part of this publication may be reproduced without the written permission of the author.

This is a work of fiction. Names and characters are either the product of the author's imagination or are used fictitiously, and any resemblance to actual persons, living or dead, business establishments, events, or locales is entirely coincidental.

Created with Vellum

I

"The house looks amazing, Mom." I stood in the center of her living room and looked around the spacious cottage. "I can't believe Stryker Construction got this place built in two months."

When Mom made her big announcement back in February that she was building a cottage between my castle and Black Forest to be closer to Dad...well, to say I was surprised, would be an understatement. For most of my life, Mom had stayed away from my dad—claiming it was just too painful. But something had happened over the last year since my return to Enchanted Island, and now Mom was spending more time in Black Forest and with my dad.

"They did a great job," Mom said. "They were even able to get all my upgrades in on time."

I laughed. "Well, when you have two werewolves, a vampire, and a witch doing the job, anything is possible."

"I love the woodwork around all your doors," Zoie said.

Zoie Stone—witch and gargoyle shifter—was a junior in

high school, and my fiancé Alex's daughter. They'd both recently moved in with me, and I couldn't be happier.

"I went with a craftsman-style cottage for that very reason." Mom gave a small laugh. "With all the plants and wood throughout, it makes me feel like the forest is inside my home.

My cousin, Serena, took a sip of her water. Now that she was pregnant, that was her drink of choice. "And is it true some of the wood came from Black Forest?"

"It sure did," Mom said. "He insisted I have it for added protection."

My dad, Black Forest King, had grown increasingly worried over the last year at the rise in violence and murder on our small island. Not that I blamed him—I was also alarmed. Even though I was the game warden for Enchanted Island, I still helped out Alex and Grant with criminal activity thanks to my years as a detective with the Paranormal Apprehension and Detention Agency.

"I like how you can see the living room, kitchen, and dining room," I said, "but they also seem somewhat secluded because of the wood casings. Like there's a little privacy even though you can see everything."

"Now I'm totally jealous," GiGi grumbled, her slightly wrinkled face set in a scowl. "Here Serenity has a new cottage, and Grant and Serena and baby-on-board have moved into my old place, and Shayla is living in between both those houses in her beautiful castle with Alex and Zoie. And here I am, being booted into town—some thirty minutes away." GiGi narrowed her eyes and glared at Grant and Alex. "I bet you both planned that, right?"

Both men raised their hands in the air, denying her accusation.

GiGi put her hands on her hips and leaned in close to Alex.

"So you wouldn't mind if I moved into the castle? After all, there's plenty of room."

"She moves in," Needles said, his wings glowing red, *"And I'm going AWOL. This job doesn't pay enough for me to live with GiGi."*

Everyone laughed except Mom and GiGi. They were the only ones in the room who couldn't hear Needles—a flying and talking porcupine warrior sent by my dad to watch over me. I'd always been able to hear Needles from the time I was a small child because I had a special connection to plants and animals, something I'd inherited from my dad. But a few months ago, there'd been an explosion near Serena's bakery, and now everyone at the scene had the ability to hear Needles speak—much to my fiancé's dismay.

"I take it Needles said no?" GiGi grumbled.

"That was a no," I agreed.

"Then it's a good thing I finally passed my driving test," GiGi said. "Even though I still say it's ridiculous a witch my age has to have one."

It was a long-standing argument between Alex and GiGi. She'd ridden her Vespa around the island since before I was born with no license. But Alex was the sheriff for Enchanted Island, and Grant was a detective. According to them, GiGi now needed a license.

Alex pressed his lips together and frowned. "It's the law, GiGi."

GiGi crossed her arms over her chest and glared at Alex. "It's ridiculous."

When Alex didn't rise to her bait anymore, GiGi grinned triumphantly and took a sip of her wine.

"Are you finding the drive to town easier to do?" Mom asked

Serena as she motioned for us to all sit and help ourselves to the snack food she'd made.

Serena nibbled on a cookie before answering. "Yes. At first, it was a little tough driving the extra thirty minutes to town, especially when I'm at the bakery by four-thirty every morning. But now I'm enjoying the drive. Gives me some quiet time to think."

We all lived on the northeast side of the island near Black Forest, and we were the only people around for a good ten miles. No one built on the north side of the island—it was Dad's only rule to living on Enchanted Island. But that was okay because the island was still big enough to house all the trees and animals and still have room for the myriad supernaturals who lived on it.

"What about you, Zoie?" Grant asked. "Do you feel seventeen yet?"

Zoie shoved the last of a cookie in her mouth, then shrugged. "Nah. I don't suppose I'll feel any differently until I hit eighteen." She sent her dad a mischievous grin. "Then I'll be an adult, *and* I'll be about to graduate from high school."

Alex winced and smacked his hand against his chest. "Don't talk like that, Zoie. I'm not ready."

I rested my head against his shoulder. "You still have time to get used to it."

"Isn't prom in a couple days?" GiGi asked.

"Two days," Zoie said, "and I can't wait. My dress is *amazing*, and Shayla and Serena are going to do my hair like they did for the last dance. All I have to do is get Brick's flower."

"I'll pick up his boutonniere for you tomorrow," I said. "I have to drop off my latest reports to Mayor Stone regarding my findings on the north side of the island."

I was the game warden for Enchanted Island, and because of that, Dad had given me special permission to hike the vastness that made up the north side of the island and catalog my findings.

"Thanks, Shayla," Zoie said. "I'd appreciate it."

"Speaking of Friday," Serena said. "What are you wearing to Charlotte's going away party? I've hit my second trimester and feel like a blimp."

"You look beautiful," Grant assured her, giving her a kiss on the cheek.

"Where's your friend moving to?" Zoie asked.

Charlotte Stoneman was an elemental witch who ran a jewelry shop in town with her cousin, Annaleigh. The girls designed their own jewelry, and then Charlotte charmed the stones and gems.

"She's moving to Hollow Springs," Serena said. "She met this guy at a gemstone convention about six months ago, and they totally hit it off. He's also an elemental witch and has a profitable store where he lives, and so she's moving there to be near him and work in his shop."

"What about her store in town?" Mom asked. "Have you heard what will happen with it?"

Serena shook her head. "I guess Annaleigh will take over, or Charlotte may sell the building. I haven't really heard."

GiGi frowned. "Can Annaleigh do magic like Charlotte? I thought she was a Normal?"

Normals were what we called supernaturals who were born into magical families but who couldn't shift or do magic of any kind.

Serena nodded. "She's a Normal. But I know she helps with the jewelry making, so maybe she'll just switch the store to a non-magical jewelry shop."

"I bet Annaleigh is heartbroken," Mom said.

Serena nodded. "She and Charlotte were raised together like we were, Shayla. I remember when you left the island to join the supernatural police academy…I was crushed. I may have only been eight, but you'd been my best friend up until that time." Serena wiped away a tear and gave a shaky laugh. "These damn hormones. I only meant it will be hard on Annaleigh."

Grant pulled Serena close and kissed her temple.

"Do Charlotte's parents live on Enchanted Island?" Alex asked, leaning over to grab an elderberry scone off the tray.

"No," Serena said. "They were killed when Charlotte was still in high school. Charlotte and Annaleigh are my age more than Shayla's. I was a senior, and the two cousins were juniors when it happened."

"So they're close in age," Zoie said.

Serena nodded. "Only six months apart."

"When Charlotte's parents died," Mom said, "she moved in with Annaleigh and her mother. The girls started making jewelry after graduation, and a few years back, Charlotte bought a store in town using the inheritance from her parents' life insurance policy."

Serena snatched the last bite of cookie from Grant's hand and shoved it in her mouth. He just laughed, shook his head, and leaned down to get another. Breaking the cookie, he gave her half.

Mom picked up her glass of wine off the end table. "It will be hard for Annaleigh to lose not only her best friend and business partner, but to also lose the business as well—at least, the magical part of it…" Her voice trailed off. "Well, it'll be tough."

"Annaleigh's mom couldn't charm the stones for her?" Zoie asked.

Serena shook her head. "Charlotte got her elemental magic from her dad's side. Euthelva—Annaleigh's mom—can't do that kind of magic. I'm afraid Charming Baubles will just go out of business."

"Back to your original question of what I'm wearing to the

party," I said, trying to lighten the mood. "I believe I'll wear my olive green dress tomorrow night."

Serena whistled. "Fancy."

I laughed. "Not really. It's the most comfortable dress I own. Nice and flowy."

"Where's the party going to be?" Zoie asked.

I grinned. "At Boos & Brews."

My childhood friend, Tommy Trollman, owned the wildly popular bar. Much to Alex's dismay, Tommy was not only a local businessman, but my troll friend was also a loan shark of sorts. At least, that was what Alex called him. I called him a godsend when the banks said no. Deep down, Tommy had a heart of gold and was honestly interested in helping the citizens of Enchanted Island. He'd offered to hold Serena's bachelorette party in his back room for us at no charge a few months back, and he was always willing to help with information when I asked.

Zoie clapped her hands in excitement. "You guys will have so much fun."

Alex draped his arm around the back of the sofa and smiled at me. "Just promise me there won't be any excitement like there was at Serena's bachelorette party."

"I'd promise," I said, giving him a wink, "but you know I can't guarantee anything."

2

"I'll just wait in the Bronco,"* Needles grumbled from the front seat the next morning. *"I'm starving. I hope you plan on feeding me soon."*

I scoffed and grabbed my file from the backseat. "I know for a fact Zoie slipped you a couple pretzels as she was leaving for school this morning."

"They wore off on the drive into town."

I rolled my eyes. "Fine. We'll stop by the bakery after this."

City Hall was deserted when I walked inside. In fact, the secretary, Daisy Woods, wasn't even behind her desk. Luckily, the mayor's door was open, so I went on in.

"What's new on the north side of the island?" Mayor Stone asked.

It didn't take long for me to go over my charts and reports on the latest findings regarding the fish population in a lagoon I'd recently discovered, as well as the list of rare plants I'd spotted.

"This is all great work," he said. "Can't wait to hear what you'll discover next."

With a promise to keep him posted, I headed back out to the lobby.

"Sorry I missed you," Daisy said from behind her desk as I crossed the foyer of City Hall. "I was getting a cup of coffee when you came in."

"That's okay. The mayor's door was open, so I just went on in."

"So, are you and Serena going to Charlotte's going away party tonight?"

"Yes. Are you?"

"Of course. Not much else to do on the island."

I laughed. "You're right about that."

"I just feel so sorry for Annaleigh."

"I'm sure everything will work out," I said. "Have you heard what's going to happen to the jewelry shop?"

Daisy's eyes went wide. "I heard Charlotte is selling the building. Can you believe it? I thought maybe Annaleigh would just continue making her jewelry and sell it from the store, but I guess not."

"That's too bad."

"I know. I loved shopping at Charming Baubles." Daisy rolled up on the balls of her feet. "Well, I guess I'll see you tonight."

I gave her a wave and headed outside. If what Daisy said was true and Charlotte really was selling her building, then Annaleigh must be devastated.

"About time," Needles grumbled, his wings glowing red. *"I passed out earlier from hunger, but the rumble of my stomach woke me up."*

"You're *such* a drama queen, Needles. You seriously missed your calling. Instead of a warrior, you should have been an actor."

Needles huffed and crossed his tiny paws over his chest—or at least he tried to. *"Just drive, Princess."*

Grinning, I pulled out onto the street and cut down a back alleyway to get to the bakery faster. I'd just pulled out onto Charm Street and was about to turn left when something caught my eye. Charlotte Stoneman was standing in front of her store talking to Grey Wolfstein, the werewolf business owner next door. Charlotte pointed to her sign, and Grey nodded.

I parked my Bronco outside Enchanted Bakery & Brew and strolled inside. Since it was a little after ten, the bakery was pretty quiet. I waved to Serena and Tamara behind the counter, then greeted a couple other customers sitting at tables. Needles zipped ahead of me to the counter and waited impatiently for me to order.

"I'll have a large coffee, elderberry muffin, and a caramel-dipped pretzel for Needles."

While Serena filled my order, I told the girls what I'd just seen outside Charlotte's store.

"So does that mean Grey is buying the building?" Serena mused. "Maybe he plans on expanding his shop. I know Enchanted Appliances Plus has been looking to expand."

"Poor Annaleigh," Tamara said. "Wonder what she'll do now?"

"No idea." I pointed to the chocolate chip cookies in the display case. "Throw in half a dozen, would ya? I have to run to Iris' flower shop and pick up Zoie's boutonniere. Iris might need some sugar to get her through the prom rush."

Serena laughed. "Good thinking."

"And maybe some wine," Tamara added.

Serena handed me my coffee and two bags of goodies. Waving goodbye, Needles and I headed back outside.

"Forever Flowers is within walking distance," I said.

"I think I'll just sit on the roof of your vehicle and eat my caramel pretzel stick and be on the lookout for bad guys."

I snorted. "I figured you'd say that."

After setting my coffee and muffin inside the Bronco, I crossed the street and strolled down to Iris' flower shop. When I opened the door, the bell overhead jingled, causing Iris to look up and wave. I loved walking into Iris' shop. The immediate connection I had to the plants inside always lifted my spirits. I could feel their emotions, and they were always happy and healthy.

I chuckled when I noticed five women already waiting in line at the counter. They were probably there picking up flowers for their kids' prom dates, just like I was. The cookies I'd brought were definitely going to come in handy.

"Hello, Shayla."

I turned and blinked in surprise at Annaleigh Hexly standing behind me. "Hey, Annaleigh. Are you picking up prom flowers too?"

Annaleigh shook her head and laughed, her auburn hair moving with her. "Goodness, no. I'm here picking up centerpieces for tonight's party. I wasn't thinking when I placed my order with Iris last week how crazy busy she'd be. When you're out of school and have no kids, you sort of lose track with that stuff."

I nodded. "Until Zoie came into my life, I never thought about school events. Now, I'm juggling work and the social life of a teenager."

"You're lucky. I'd give anything to find someone I could settle down with and have kids. I'm so ready for that part of my life to happen." Annaleigh shrugged. "I can't help but be a little jealous of Charlotte. Of course, I love Enchanted Island, and I never want to leave...but, it may come to that if I can't find an eligible bachelor soon."

I bit my lip and grimaced. "I hate to bring this up if it's too painful, but I drove by Charming Baubles earlier and saw Charlotte talking to Grey Wolfstein. Is he thinking of buying the building?"

Annaleigh sighed. "Yes. He's wanting to expand his appliance store."

"You okay with that happening?" I asked.

Something flickered in Annaleigh's eyes, but it was gone before I could pinpoint the emotion.

"It's her store," Annaleigh said. "She bought it and made it what it is." She flipped her hair over her shoulders. "Not much I can do about it. Everyone knows I can't work magic, so there's no way I can take over for her." She cleared her throat and smiled. "But it's what Charlotte wants. She's excited to start this next chapter of her life with James, and I can't blame her."

"It's too bad James can't move to Enchanted Island."

"Yeah, but he already has a business established where he is, and Hollow Springs is three times the size of Enchanted Island, so there're more customers for Charlotte to sell to." Annaleigh looked around the shop, then leaned in close. "Besides, I think there's a part of Charlotte that's happy to leave here because of Beau. Their breakup was awful, and he's still not over it."

My brows furrowed. "I wasn't aware Charlotte was dating someone else."

"Oh, that's right. You've been gone for a long time. Charlotte and Beau dated for like a year. Then about ten months ago, they broke up. And the truth is, Beau's never gotten over it." She shrugged and crossed her arms over her chest. "I've told Charlotte a ton of times she should call the cops on him. Sometimes he'll follow her when she goes out on the weekends, or he'll pretend he just happened to show up where she is. There were even times before she met James when she *tried* to go on a date, and Beau would threaten the guys. It's absolutely insane. So I'm glad Charlotte could find someone off the island to fall in love with. Could you imagine if she had to stay here with Beau being all stalkerish?"

"That's horrible. And, yes, she should have called the police on him."

"Well, I better go grab my flowers out of the case. Lucia Trollski and I are going over to Boos & Brews around two to decorate early. See you at seven."

"See you then, Annaleigh."

* * *

"How do they look?" Zoie sprinted into my kitchen and shoved her hands in my face. "Izzy and I went to Magical Nails after school and had our nails done for prom tomorrow."

I backed up so I could get a good look at the colorful nails inches from my eyes. "Impressive. Love the color."

"I figured since my dress was red with gobs of rhinestones, my nails should also look like that."

"You could kill someone with those talons," Needles said, his wings glowing the same color as Zoie's nails. *"I wholeheartedly approve."*

Zoie and I both laughed.

"I'm making lobster rolls and salad for dinner," I said, strolling back to the counter.

Zoie waved her hand through the air, using her magic to open the refrigerator and get out a can of cold coffee. Not wanting to ruin her nails, she also used her magic to open the tab.

"Nice," I said. "I do the same thing with wine bottles sometimes."

Zoie snorted. "Good one."

"Do *not* teach my teenager how to open wine bottles using magic," Alex said as he strode into the kitchen, still wearing his Sheriff's uniform. "I have enough to worry about."

"Like she hasn't tried already," Needles snickered.

Alex shot Needles a death glare before turning to me. "Dinner looks good."

"Lobster rolls and salad. I'm walking down to Serena's around six-thirty, and then she's driving to the party tonight since she can't drink. Thought I'd get dinner around for you guys beforehand."

"I'm just staying in tonight," Zoie said. "I told Brick there was no need to go out and spend money tonight since we have prom tomorrow."

"Speaking of," I said. "Your boutonniere is in the refrigerator."

Zoie ran over and gave me a squeeze around my waist. "Thanks, Shayla."

"Yes, thanks." Alex untwisted the top of a beer bottle and gave me a wink. "I owe you one."

"I'm gonna go pack before dinner," Zoie said.

"Pack for what?" Alex asked.

Zoie rolled her eyes. "Dad, you know I'm spending the night with Izzy tomorrow after prom. We talked about this."

"Oh, yeah. I remember."

"Liar," I whispered.

Zoie exited the kitchen, Needles chatting away near her shoulder.

"I'm still nervous about this prom thing," Alex said. "Especially since she has a date. I mean, I know Brick and Zoie have been dating for a while, but there's just something about prom night that makes me…well, now that I'm a father, it makes my stomach hurt."

I chuckled. "That's because you remember what *you* were like at Brick's age."

Alex wrapped his arms around me and buried his head in my neck. "You aren't wrong. But now that I have a daughter, it's a different story."

"She's a good kid. She'll use her head and be safe."

"That's what I'm counting on."

3

"Everyone gets a name tag," Annaleigh sang out as a group of us strolled through the back door of Boos & Brews a little after seven o'clock. The room was filled with hundreds of balloons and a massive banner that read, "We Will Miss You, Charlotte."

Groaning, I wrote my name on the white paper, peeled off the backing, then plastered it to my dress. Handing the pen to Serena, she quickly did the same.

We dropped off our going-away card at the designated table, then stopped to talk to a group of witches for a while before finally making our way over to the refreshment table. Serena made quick work of her plate full of petit fours, and I couldn't resist teasing her.

"Did you breathe?" I joked.

She quickly blinked back tears. "I know! At this rate, I'm going to be as big as a house."

"Hey, I was only teasing."

"I know, I know. It's these darn hormones and mood swings.

Poor Grant is afraid to speak to me half the time because I can't seem to do anything but bite off his head."

I grinned. "Once the baby comes, you'll forget all about these weird body things and just focus on the werewitch."

Serena laughed. "I hope you're right."

"Let's grab a drink," I said. "You want—oops, sorry. I keep forgetting."

Serena laughed and patted her baby bump. "Trust me, this werewitch doesn't need any extra kick—he or she has plenty as it is."

We ambled over to a makeshift counter where drinks were being served. I smiled at the older woman in front of me, waiting on her glass of punch. She was dressed in all black, which was a striking contrast to the silver-blonde bob she sported.

Her sky-blue eyes held mine as I pointed to the punch bowl. "Is it spiked? Do you know?"

"It's not spiked." She looked down at my name tag. "Oh, Shayla. You probably don't remember me. I haven't seen you since you returned to the island. I'm Euthelva…Annaleigh's mother."

"Oh, right." I stuck out my hand. "How are you?"

"Can't complain. Sad to see Charlotte go, but I guess it's what she wants."

"I suppose it is." I gestured to Serena. "I thought I should scope out the punch for the mom-to-be."

Euthelva's eyes dropped to Serena's stomach. "Congratulations."

"Thanks." Serena placed a hand over her slightly swollen belly. "Grant and I are excited."

Euthelva smiled. "Lots of good fortune happening to folks lately. Hope everything is going well so far?"

"It is." Serena caressed her stomach in a circular motion. "Just hit my second trimester about three weeks ago."

Euthelva nodded. "I remember the second trimester well. Be sure to sign the slab of slate over on the table by the balloons. A sort of going-away present Charlotte can take with her."

"We'll do that," Serena said.

"What can I get you?" the woman behind the counter asked.

"I need one glass of punch," I said. "Then I'll take a glass of whatever white you're serving."

"Have fun tonight, ladies," Euthelva said before turning and walking away.

Once our drinks were in hand, Serena and I headed over to where Finn Faeton stood. Finn was the island's forensic scientist, but you'd never know it to look at her. The girl loved color, as was evidenced by her multi-colored hair, colorful tattoos, bright clothes, and myriad piercings containing colored gems.

"Finally!" Finn said. "Someone I can talk to. I know a lot of these people, but it's not like we hang out much."

"What's in your glass?" I asked. "It looks yummy and shimmery."

"It's called Bye-Bye Berry, and it's the nightly special, according to Tommy. It has two different berry vodkas with a splash of seltzer and edible glitter." She held the drink up to the light, and we all watched as the glittery red liquid swirled in a clockwise motion. "Isn't it stunning?"

"Sure is," Serena said. "First drink I'm trying after the baby."

Finn laughed and took a sip, sighing in delight. "Delicious. Is Tamara coming?"

Serena shook her head. "No. She's watching Baby Jayden until Zac finishes his shift around nine tonight."

Finn grinned and poked me in the ribs. "First Tamara gets

tamed by a baby, and now Serena is pregnant. Looks like it's up to you and me to keep the party going."

I laughed and shook my head. "Oh, no. My party days are over. Heck, I'm not even sure I ever had party days. But trust me, at forty, they're over. It takes me two days just to recover from one glass of wine too many."

"Guess it's just up to me." Finn tossed back the last of her Bye-Bye Berry drink. "I hate to jinx anything, but it's been pretty quiet around the island the last month and a half. No big cases outside of some burglaries and the normal drunk and disorderly fighting stuff."

I took a sip of my wine. "I know. Hope it stays that way."

"Thank you for coming," Annaleigh said as she sidled up next to us. "Don't forget to sign your name on Charlotte's goodbye slate."

"We'll be sure to do that," Serena said. "Everything looks wonderful, Annaleigh. You did a great job decorating."

"Didn't she?" Charlotte mused as she joined our group and hugged her cousin around the waist. "I told her not to go to all this trouble, but she just wouldn't listen."

"I'm your cousin, and you are leaving the island. I'm supposed to make a big fuss."

Charlotte rested her head on Annaleigh's shoulder. "You're the best. I'm going to miss you so much."

"And I'm going to miss you," Annaleigh murmured.

"It's a great turnout," I said. "Looks like we won't be the only ones to miss you."

"I know!" Charlotte exclaimed. "I think I counted like sixty or seventy people here already. And the night is just getting started. The DJ is about done setting up, so we should be dancing soon."

"Sounds like fun," I lied.

Serena choked on her punch. She knew me too well to think I actually meant I couldn't wait to dance.

"You okay?" Annaleigh asked.

Serena nodded. "Yes, just went down the wrong pipe."

"I'm going to get me another Bye-Bye Berry," Finn said. "Anyone else need a drink?"

We all shook our heads.

"Hold my spot," Finn joked. "I'll be back in—"

She was cut off as angry voices reached us. We all turned and strained to see what was going on, and I heard Charlotte and Annaleigh both gasp.

"What's *she* doing here?" Annaleigh demanded.

"Who is it?" I asked.

"Ellen Vampton," Charlotte said.

"I take it you two aren't friendly?" I asked, watching with amusement as the diminutive Ellen did her best to get by Lucia, a giant female troll, blocking her way.

Charlotte sighed. "Let's just say Ellen has a lot of anger and animosity towards me. She blames me for things out of my control."

"Someone needs to call her husband," Annaleigh snapped. "Have him drag her home." Annaleigh shoved her drink at Charlotte. "Hold this. I'm going over there and throwing her butt out."

"Looks like Lucia has it under control," Finn said.

Lucia, standing over six feet tall and towering over most of the crowd, wasn't having any of Ellen's antics. When the smaller woman finally darted past the troll, Lucia reached out, grabbed the back of Ellen's shirt, and yanked her backward. Ellen screamed, her arms flailing backward as Lucia dragged her toward the back door.

"We better try to smooth this out," Charlotte said.

Annaleigh sighed. "If we must. I'm sorry you all

had to see that. Go fill your glasses and then hit the dance floor."

We waited until Charlotte and Annaleigh walked away before talking over each other.

"What the heck was that about?"

"Who was that woman?"

"We've *got* to know the rest of the story."

I held up my hand to stop our collective chatter. "Euthelva is over by the slate thing we're supposed to sign, talking with some women. Maybe she can tell us something."

We pushed our way through the throng of bodies. Most had gone back to chatting and drinking, and now that the DJ was playing music, a few were migrating toward the small makeshift dance floor near the front of the room.

When we reached the table that held the slab of slate stone, Serena picked up the pen and started to write her well wishes.

As she did, I tapped Euthelva on the shoulder. "I hope everything is okay. I saw that scuffle by the back door."

Euthelva sighed and took a drink of her wine. "Everything's fine. Just typical Ellen making a scene."

"Does Ellen do this a lot?" I asked.

"Yes, she does. But nobody really listens to her anymore. She's just a bitter witch who enjoys making others miserable."

I was going to ask another question, but Euthelva turned her back to me and joined the conversation she'd been having with her friends before I interrupted.

Finn and I quickly scribbled our names on the slate next to Serena's, then headed over to the drink table. Since I wasn't driving, I figured I might as well make the most of the night.

We were almost at the booze table when Lucia Trollski stopped us.

"Serena," Lucia said. "I was wondering if you and Shayla might help with cleanup after the party? The more witches we have to help, the faster it will go."

I surreptitiously glanced at my watch and stifled a groan. We still had an hour before the party ended, but I knew Serena couldn't say no.

Serena glanced at me. "You okay with that, Shayla?"

I shrugged. "Sure. No problem."

Finn and I ordered the Bye-Bye Berry, and pretty soon I'd loosened up enough to dance. At some point, Daisy Woods joined us on the dance floor, and before I knew it, the hour was up, and all the ladies were gathering their belongings to go home.

"I'm calling it a night," Finn said.

"Me too." Daisy slurped down the last of her Bye-Bye Berry and giggled. "This was *really* good."

"You okay to drive home?" I asked Daisy.

"Oh, I'm catching a ride with a couple friends."

Serena groaned and clutched her lower back. "I hate to run off, but I have to use the bathroom again."

Laughing, I looped my arm around hers. "I'll go with you."

We said goodnight to Daisy and Finn and were almost to the bathroom when I saw Euthelva yelling at a tall man by the back door. He was wearing one of the name tags we'd all had to don, but he was too far away for me to read his name.

"Who's that?" I asked.

"That's Beau Broombotten," Serena said. "Charlotte's ex-boyfriend."

I let out a bark of laughter. "Broombottom? Seriously? That's his last name?"

Serena pressed her lips together and tried not to smile, but she finally gave in and laughed along with me. "It's Broom*botten*. And, yes, I know. How unfortunate. His family isn't from the island. I think he moved here like eight or nine years ago. Well after you left."

I glanced across the almost-empty room and saw Charlotte huddled next to Lucia. Both women watched intently as Euthelva pointed outside. Just when I thought I was going to have to intercede, Euthelva lifted her other hand, said something I couldn't hear, and Beau flew backward out the door. The door then slammed shut on its own.

"Well," I murmured. "That's one way to get someone to leave."

4

Since there were six witches, two fairies, and one troll helping to clean up, we split up chores. Serena, Aggie, Teresa, and I stayed inside to clean while Annaleigh, Euthelva, Lucia, Darby, and Gwen packed up and hauled the boxes to the cars. Annaleigh insisted Charlotte finish saying goodbye to the stragglers, call an Uber, and then go home.

"It's your party," Annaleigh said. "You don't clean after your own party. I'll see you back home in a little while."

I'd just conjured up a vacuum when Euthelva stepped in front of me, a big box of party favors hovering in the air above us.

"Oops," she said. "Sorry about that. I was watching the box instead of where I was going."

I laughed and waved my hand, sending my vacuum to another part of the room. "No problem. You got that?"

"I do, thanks. I'll be glad when I can go home and put my feet up, though. I'm not like you youngins." She shook her head, her silver-blonde hair moving with her. "I'm so exhausted right now I could fall on my face. If I don't see you before you leave, tell your mom hello for me. And thanks for coming out to see Charlotte off."

I wished her goodnight and turned back to focus on my vacuum cleaner scooting around the room on its own. Jogging to catch up with it, I went back to vacuuming. When I finished, I moved to where Serena and Teresa were using their magic to gather up all the discarded glasses.

"We only have this section left," Serena said, "then we'll be finished."

"No hurry," I said. "How're you doing, Teresa?"

Teresa Glowburn smiled. "Pretty good. I have a big showing in New York coming up."

Teresa was a fire witch who used her gifts to blow glass and make pottery. Her pieces were popular in both the human and supernatural worlds.

"Euthelva says that's everything," Lucia said a little while later as she ambled over to us. "I think we can go."

Teresa tied off the last trash bag and handed it to Lucia. "We're finished in here as well."

"Anyone seen Charlotte?" Serena asked. "I'd like to say goodbye."

Lucia frowned and tossed the bag over one large shoulder. "Last I saw, she was going outside to call Brooms Away, I think. But that was quite a while ago. She's probably left by now."

Brooms Away was the taxi service on Enchanted Island.

"That's too bad," Serena said. "But I'm sure I can catch her before she leaves the island."

We all said goodnight, and I grabbed Serena's arm. "It's only like a quarter till ten. Let's go say goodbye to Tommy real quick."

Serena grinned. "Let's go."

I glanced down at her stomach and grimaced. "That is, if

you're sure you're up to it. I know you worked all day, then being here, and now helping to clean up…" My voice trailed off, unsure if I was putting too much on her. "We don't have to."

Serena snorted and whirled me toward the door that led to the bar. "I'll tell you like I tell Grant—I'm pregnant, not fragile. *Huge* difference."

I laughed. "Good. Let's go say goodnight to Tommy."

I opened the door and led us down the small hallway that ended at Tommy's office. Loud voices and even louder music pulsed from the bar, so I knocked extra loud on Tommy's door.

"Come in."

The voice inside was gruff and sharp. Pushing open the door, Serena and I stepped inside. When Tommy saw us, his wide face split into a grin.

"I was hoping you might stop by and say hello." He stood and walked around his desk. Like most trolls, he was exceptionally tall and solidly built. "You both look lovely." He leaned down and kissed us each on the cheek. "Have fun?"

I laughed. "With Bye-Bye Berry, how could we not?"

He threw back his head and laughed. "I thought you ladies might enjoy." When he looked down at Serena, his face softened. "I hear congratulations are in order. When's the baby due?"

Serena huffed and crossed her arms over her chest. "About a week before Shayla's wedding. I'm gonna look ridiculous in a bridesmaid dress."

I rolled my eyes and wrapped my arm around her shoulder. "Oh, please. You could never look ridiculous in anything."

Tommy gestured for us to sit down. Outside of Serena—who was ten years younger than me—I hadn't had many friends growing up. When your dad was Black Forest King…well, it wasn't always easy. Tommy had been my first true friend outside of family, and we'd always shared a special bond.

We spent the next few minutes catching up and sharing stories, until a sudden knock on the door brought us up short.

"Yes?" Tommy called out.

The door opened, and a man poked his head inside. "Sorry, Boss. Got a rowdy vampire group I thought you might need to deal with."

Tommy sighed and rose from behind his desk. "I'll be right out." He looked down at me and smiled. "I need to see to my bar. It's been nice catching up. You tell Sheriff Stone I said hello."

My lips twitched at that. Alex may still have issues regarding Tommy's "side job" on the island, but after Tommy explained a few things about how their families were actually intertwined—Alex had a new appreciation for Tommy and his desire to help the other citizens of Enchanted Island who needed a hand up.

"I'll definitely tell Alex you said hello." I stood on my tiptoe and kissed his cheek. "Thanks for everything, Tommy."

He opened the door for us, and Serena and I pushed our way through the throng of people and exited out the front door of Boos & Brews.

Breathing in the fresh air, I looped my arm around Serena's. "Let's go home. I'm exhausted."

Serena bumped her hip against mine. "Ditto. How can it only be ten, and I'm ready to drop?"

"Because you run a successful bakery where you're up every morning by three-thirty, and now you have *another* bun in the oven to care for."

Serena groaned as we headed down the side alley to the back parking lot where her car was located. "How long have you been waiting to say that?"

I grinned. "A long time. Bun in the oven." I threw back my head and laughed. "Good one, right?"

"Yes." We sidestepped a pothole, still giggling. "Tamara told me not to come in until six tomorrow, but I just can't do that."

We came to the end of the alley and turned right. The back parking lot was mainly for workers and people using the back room. There were a few streetlights illuminating the lot, but most of the cars were encased in darkness.

"Do you want me to drive home?" I asked. "I only had two drinks in three hours. I'm good."

"I can drive. I'm not *that* tired."

A loud screech brought us up short.

"What was that?" Serena demanded.

My instincts were immediately on alert as a stab of sorrow shot through me. "It's a cat. I think it's…hurt or something. Stay here."

I headed toward the dumpster, opening my mind to the emotions of the animal. If he *was* hurt, he might be scared and attack.

"I'm sure it's nothing," Serena called, "but be careful, just in case."

I crept past the other seven cars in the lot and threw up a light orb as I neared the back fence. When I was about three feet away from the dumpster, I let out a cry of surprise—making the cat bolt.

"What? What is it?" Serena asked, panic in her voice.

"Call Grant and Alex."

"Oh, no. What happened?"

I heard the clack of her shoes and knew she was walking toward me.

"Don't come any closer." I turned to face her. "You don't want to see this."

"Who?"

I sighed. "It's Charlotte. She's dead."

5

"It's bad." Alex and Grant strode toward me as I backed away from the dumpster. "I didn't touch the body yet, though."

Deputy Sparks, who'd already been on duty, was inside getting statements from the workers whose cars were still in the back lot. Tommy Trollman stood with his back against the building, hands in his pockets. Since it had taken less than fifteen minutes for the guys to get to town, I knew Alex must have shifted into his gargoyle form and flown them in.

"I called Finn and told her to just stay home," I said. "We'd bag and tag everything for her to pour over in the morning. But Doc should be here shortly."

"Where's Serena?" Grant demanded.

"She's sitting in her car over there," I said, pointing to Serena's car on the other side of the lot. "I didn't want her around this."

Grant turned and strode toward Serena's car as Alex sidled up next to me.

"What have you got?" he asked.

I looked down at Charlotte's body and pushed aside the bubbling emotion. "It's Charlotte Stoneman." I crouched and motioned for him to do the same. "And it's bad, Alex. If I had to guess, I'd say her larynx was crushed." I sighed. "And I can smell magic. Not so much now, but when I first discovered her, there were traces of it coming from her mouth."

"Meaning?"

I looked him in the eyes. "Death spell."

Alex inhaled sharply. "Seriously? Like the Sleeping Beauty spell we encountered a while back?"

"Sort of."

"How did you find her back behind the dumpster?"

"An alley cat alerted me. He'd let out a pitiful cry, and sadness and pain immediately flooded my body. I knew something was wrong, so I came to see."

"Can you conjure me up a pair of gloves? I left the house without grabbing any."

Using my magic, I quickly did as he requested.

"Thanks." He shoved his hands in the latex gloves. "Have you taken pictures?"

I nodded. "I have about a hundred of them on my phone. I looked under the dumpster as best I could in this dress, but I didn't see anything."

Lying flat on his stomach, Alex searched the underside for himself. "Can you give me some light?"

I brought the light orb I'd conjured up earlier closer to him, then sat back on my heels as Alex inspected under the dumpster, and then moved to inspect Charlotte's body.

"She's got something in her hand." Alex turned and showed me a piece of paper in his gloved hand. "Recognize it."

I glanced down at my own name tag. "Annaleigh had us all

wear one tonight." I sighed. "Guess that means the killer was someone at the party. I hate this."

I conjured up an evidence bag, and Alex placed the torn corner of the name tag in the bag.

"If we're lucky," he said, "there might be fingerprints on that specific section."

It was a long shot, but luck could be on our side. Once Alex had finished processing the scene, we both stood back from the body.

"I'm sorry about your friend."

"Thanks. She was really more Serena's friend than mine, but she was a kind woman, and this is going to crush her cousin."

"Any idea who at the party might want her dead?"

I sighed. "I saw her—well, *Charlotte* didn't really have words with these two individuals, but I know there were hard feelings. One was Ellen Vampton, and the other was Beau Broombotten.

Alex stared at me. "You're kidding, right? Broombottom?"

I laughed softly. "I said the same thing. It's actually Broom*botten*. B-o-t-t-e-n."

"I bet his childhood was tough."

I let out another shaky laugh. "He's not from the island, so I don't know much about him."

"And Ellen Vampton? Do you know her?"

"Not really. I didn't ask what her maiden name was, but I got the impression she and her husband were having issues, and Ellen blamed Charlotte."

"Affair?"

"I don't think so. It was more Ellen blamed Charlotte for not giving her something or making something happen for her. I didn't really get an answer to that question during the exchange."

"Anyone else?"

I glanced over at Tommy, who was now talking on his phone. "Maybe her cousin? And not because of anything that happened tonight. I just know Charlotte is selling her building to Grey Wolfstein and closing her business."

"Which means Annaleigh will be out of a job?"

I nodded. "Exactly."

Alex glanced up at the building, then swiveled his head to look around the dimly lit parking lot. "Don't suppose there are any cameras?"

"Nope."

Alex scoffed. "Of course not. That would be too easy."

"I got here as fast as I could." Doc Drago, the island's medical examiner, sidled up to us. "Tentative identification is for Charlotte Stoneman?"

"Yep. Serena and I were leaving the party when we found her."

"That's too bad." He pushed past us and put on his gloves, smiling at the light orb floating near his head. "Thanks for the added light, Shayla. Now, let's see what we got." It didn't take long before he glanced back over his shoulder at me. "Do I detect a death spell?"

I nodded. "I think so. I could smell a little dark magic still on her when I found her."

Shaking his head, Doc stood and yanked off his gloves. "Vile. Absolutely disgusting that someone would do something like this to such a lovely woman. That takes a lot of hatred and rage."

"How so?" Alex asked.

"A death spell involves dark magic," I explained. "Plus, it requires the killer to be close to the victim. Proximity is a must for this spell."

"So Charlotte saw her killer?" Alex mused.

"Definitely," Doc said. "And then the killer slowly crushed her windpipe, using magic until she died."

Alex cursed. "This is going to be a nightmare. Who can perform a spell like that?"

I shrugged. "Truthfully? I guess anyone who knows how to do a little dark magic. I don't think the spell itself is difficult, it's just not a spell a witch would normally perform. Dark magic is a no-no on Enchanted Island."

"What can I do?" Grant asked, walking up behind us.

"I don't think anything tonight," Alex said. "Shayla gave me a couple names of possible suspects you can run tomorrow. But for tonight, just take Serena home. It's late, and I know she has to be tired."

Grant nodded and clasped Alex's shoulder. "Thanks. Send me the names, and I'll run them first thing in the morning."

As Grant strolled away, Doc turned to us.

"I think I'm ready to take the body." He motioned for a paramedic to bring over the gurney. "I'll have something for you both around lunchtime. That is, if Shayla is helping work the case?"

"I'm helping," I said quickly. "I just gave my reports to the mayor today, so I'm due a couple days off. It's the least I can do for Charlotte."

Alex nodded. "That's fine by me."

"Let me levitate her body for you to the gurney," I said. "This way we don't contaminate the scene anymore, and Alex can block off the area with tape."

I conjured up crime scene tape and tossed it to Alex, then whispered a levitation spell and carefully moved Charlotte a couple feet to the gurney. When I placed her gently on the board, the paramedic nodded and headed for the back of Doc's vehicle.

As Serena's headlights backed out of the alley, Alex and I headed toward Tommy. The paramedic had just lifted Charlotte's body into the back of Doc's vehicle when the backdoor to Boos & Brews flew open and Annaleigh and Euthelva barreled outside.

"What's going on?" Euthelva demanded. "Charlotte wasn't home when Annaleigh went to their cottage. In a panic, we started making phone calls, and someone said their sister was at Boos & Brews and she claimed a deputy was inside asking questions, and that someone else was whispering Charlotte was found dead in the back parking lot. Is it true? Where's Charlotte?"

6

Alex held up his hand. "I need you two to stop where you are. No one is allowed back here except for authorized personnel."

"He's here," Annaleigh said, her voice rising an octave as she pointed to Tommy. "Does that mean it's true? Something bad happened to Charlotte back here?"

"Do you want to take this to my office?" Tommy asked.

Alex nodded. "If you don't mind. I can—"

Euthelva screamed, cutting off Alex. "Is that Charlotte under the sheet?"

The two women took off for the gurney. I held up my hands, whispered the word I used to erect an invisible shield, and the two women immediately bounced off the shield and cursed.

"Ladies," Alex said sharply. "I understand you're upset, but this isn't helping Charlotte."

"Can we *please* just see her?" Euthelva pleaded, tears running down her cheeks. "I need to see my niece for myself."

Alex nodded to Doc, who slowly lowered the sheet enough

for the two weeping women to see. When they hugged each other and continued weeping, Doc quickly covered Charlotte back up, and he and the paramedic finished lifting the gurney inside the vehicle.

"Wait," Annaleigh called out. "Where's her necklace? I didn't see it around her neck. She always wears her necklace. I know for a fact she had it on tonight during the party. It's a necklace she charmed herself after her parents died."

"It could be it broke off and is lodged in her clothes," Alex said. "Doc will look for it. Let's all go inside and talk."

"I just don't understand," Annaleigh said. "I mean, we just saw her like an hour ago."

"I think I'll close the bar early," Tommy said. "Shayla, you know where my office is. Why don't you escort these ladies there, and I'll be in as soon as I get everyone out of the bar."

Euthelva dabbed at her eyes as Tommy held open the back door. "This is just unreal."

I turned to Alex. "I'll get them settled in Tommy's office for you."

Alex nodded. "Thanks. Officer Sparks should be done interviewing the staff by now. I'll check with him and see if he has anything to report and give him the name tag evidence to log in back at the station."

I stepped inside the banquet room and followed Annaleigh, Euthelva, and Tommy across the room and out into the hallway.

"Go on to my office," Tommy said. "I'm going to get a bottle to help settle nerves. Bourbon okay?"

"Thank you," Euthelva whispered, wrapping her arm around Annaleigh's waist and continuing down the hallway.

"I'm sorry you have to shut down early on a Friday night," I said.

Tommy shrugged. "It's no big deal. I just want to help out.

Don't like murders happening in my bar." He stared me down. "I'm assuming it's a murder since her body was found behind the dumpster."

Since it wasn't really a question, I just smiled and hurried down the hall. When we reached Tommy's office, I opened the door and ushered Euthelva and Annaleigh inside.

"Why don't you guys sit on the sofa." I picked up a box of tissues from Tommy's desk and handed it to Euthelva.

"I don't understand," Euthelva said, wiping at her eyes. "Was she struck by another car? How did she die?"

"I bet it was Beau," Annaleigh said. "I bet he waited for her in the alley and killed her!"

"Let's not jump to conclusions," I said. "Doc will know more tomorrow."

"Tomorrow?" Euthelva scoffed. "We need answers tonight!"

I sighed. "I know you two are upset, and you have every right to be, but you have to let us do our jobs."

The door opened and Tommy and Alex strolled inside—Tommy carrying a tray filled with glasses and a bottle of bourbon. "Help yourselves." He set the tray down on his desk. "I'll be out in the bar area if you need me."

With a nod to me, Tommy walked out the door.

Alex poured two glasses and handed each woman a glass. "Let's just start with what all happened tonight at the party. Who attended, if anything significant happened, what time everyone left—including Charlotte—and the last thing you each saw when you left." Alex and I sat in the two club chairs in front of Tommy's desk. "Let's start with you, Euthelva."

Clutching her glass in both hands, Euthelva sat back against the cushions. "I guess if you're asking these questions, then something really bad *did* happen to Charlotte. It wasn't an accident?"

"We don't believe so," Alex said.

Euthelva closed her eyes briefly. "I guess as far as who attended, there were about sixty or seventy women here to say goodbye to Charlotte. If they signed the slate by the door when they came in, then I have those names in the back of my car. I *can* tell you there were two party crashers tonight—Ellen Vampton and Beau Broombotten. Both of them have reason to harm Charlotte."

"Do you know if those two individuals had on name tags?" Alex asked.

Euthelva frowned and looked up at the ceiling. "I guess now that you mention it, yes. I think I remember seeing that."

"I think I remember seeing Beau with one," Annaleigh said. "I'm not sure about Ellen."

"You said both of them have reason to harm Charlotte," Alex said. "What are those reasons?"

Euthelva looked sideways at Annaleigh before speaking. "Annaleigh might be able to tell you more about Ellen, since she's personally seen and had interaction with Ellen in the shop, but from what I understand, Ellen blames Charlotte for the fact she can't conceive."

I blinked in surprise. Of all the things I thought Euthelva might say…that answer never occurred to me. "Why would Ellen blame Charlotte?"

Annaleigh sighed. "Because over the last, like, eight or ten months, Ellen has commissioned Charlotte to charm at least ten pieces of jewelry for her. All with fertility spells, and none of them worked."

"And she blames Charlotte for that?" I mused.

"They were expensive pieces," Annaleigh said. "I bet she's spent over ten thousand dollars on rings, necklaces, amulets, bracelets, earrings, and even toe rings…all trying to help her get pregnant."

"That's a lot of money to spend for a fertility spell," I said.

Annaleigh shrugged. "I've never been inside her house, but I hear Ellen has fertility statues and things like that everywhere."

"So Ellen shows up at the party tonight," Alex said. "What happened then?"

"Lucia told her to leave," Annaleigh said.

"That's correct." Euthelva took a sip of her bourbon. "Then a little while later, Charlotte's ex-boyfriend, Beau, had the nerve to stroll inside like he belonged."

"That's who you need to be looking at," Annaleigh jumped in. "He's horrible. Always calling her, harassing her, stalking her. I bet what happened was he finally realized Charlotte was leaving…so he killed her!"

"Anything else out of the ordinary happen?" Alex asked.

The two women looked at each other, then shook their heads.

"How did Charlotte leave the party?" Alex asked. "Did she drive?"

"No." Annaleigh took a tiny sip of her drink and tried not to grimace. "Lucia and I came in early to decorate. This way Momma, Charlotte, and I could just all ride together."

"You three live together?" Alex asked.

"Sort of," Annaleigh said. "When things started taking off at the jewelry store, Charlotte and I had a cottage built behind Momma's place. It's close, but still gives us our own space, ya know? Anyway, after we got ready for the party, Charlotte and I walked to Momma's house, and we all drove over in Momma's car. We told Charlotte there was no way she was helping to clean up, so if we were still working by the time she told everyone goodbye, she was to call Lester at Brooms Away to take her home. Since we only live about three minutes from the bar, it wouldn't cost hardly anything."

"When was Charlotte scheduled to leave the island?" I asked.

"She's leaving on Sun—" Annaleigh broke off on a sob, and Euthelva gathered her daughter in her arms. I glanced over at Alex, who was handing the tissue box to Annaleigh.

"I'm sorry," Annaleigh whispered, dabbing at her eyes. "It just hit me I should be talking in the past tense. She's *not* leaving for the first time on Sunday to move some of her things to the mainland."

Euthelva patted Annaleigh's leg. "Charlotte was leaving Sunday. She was going to move some of her stuff and stay with James for a week or two before coming back to the island." She glanced over at her daughter. "Earlier this week, Charlotte decided to sell her building and close down her business. So she would need to come back and get the paperwork around and pick up the last of her things."

"So it's true?" I mused. "She's selling to Grey Wolfstein?"

Annaleigh nodded. "Yes. I didn't say anything earlier today because it wasn't common knowledge yet, but I guess now it's not a big deal. Charlotte told me her decision on Monday."

"And how did you react to that news, Annaleigh?" Alex mused.

"What are you saying?" Euthelva demanded.

"It's okay, Momma. I understand why he's asking." Annaleigh dropped her head and stared at her glass. "Was I upset? Yes, a little. Upset enough to kill her? Goddess, no! I *loved* Charlotte. We were like sisters." She pressed her lips together as tears ran down her cheeks. "I understood why I couldn't just step in and fill her shoes. I'm a Normal. I don't have the magic she does." She shrugged and looked at Alex.

"I've lived with that reality my entire life, Sheriff. It's not like Monday's announcement was a total shock."

Euthelva scoffed. "I loved Charlotte as well, but I just wish she would have—"

"No. We aren't doing this here, and *especially* not now." Annaleigh turned to her mother. "I mean it. I'll be just fine. I loved working with Charlotte in the store, but I don't need those four walls for me to keep making jewelry. I can sell them to the human world on the Internet. I'll be okay."

"I'm sure you will," I said, when Euthelva just pressed her lips together and nodded.

Annaleigh smiled. "Thanks, Shayla."

I shifted in my chair and leaned forward. "I was inside cleaning up after the party, so I didn't pay too much attention to what was going on around me. Did Charlotte call Brooms Away to come get her?"

Annaleigh and Euthelva looked at each other.

"I think so," Euthelva said. "But I'm not sure."

"Me, neither."

"When was the last time you saw Charlotte?" Alex asked.

Annaleigh perked up. "Oh, I remember her walking out the back door when most of the clean-up was about finished. So maybe around nine-twenty?"

"What about in the alley or back parking lot, Annaleigh?" I asked. "Did you ever see anyone back there when you were taking boxes to your mom's car?"

Annaleigh shook her head. "I don't think so."

"What about you, Euthelva?" I asked.

Euthelva bit her lip. "I'm trying to think. I'm pretty sure Charlotte told me goodnight and thanked me for the party, but I'm not sure what time it was. I made at least six trips to my car that night."

"Euthelva, do you remember when you walked in front of me?" I asked. "I was vacuuming, and you were levitating a box?"

"Of course."

"You went outside, right?"

"Yes. I took the box to my car. Like I said, I made a number of trips."

"That wasn't too long before everyone finished. You didn't see anyone outside in the parking lot?"

Euthelva shook her head. "I'm sorry. I'm just so upset. It's like everything is swimming around in my head, and I can't focus." Euthelva closed her eyes and said nothing for a few seconds. "On that trip with the box, I went straight to my car and came back inside. There wasn't anyone in the alley." Euthelva gasped. "Wait! I take it back. I was walking back inside the building because I'd just taken the box of vases out to my car. It was parked up against the fence on the far side of the parking lot. For some reason, I glanced over my shoulder and looked back toward the fence and my car and thought I saw someone." She bit her lip. "I don't know if I should say anything, just in case it wasn't him."

"Who?" Alex demanded.

Euthelva sighed. "I thought I saw—at the time I thought it was Beau—skulking around by the back fence near the side alley. He'd already been kicked out earlier. I think I yelled out something, and then Lucia walked outside, so I just went back in."

"See!" Annaleigh exclaimed. "I'm telling you, you *have* to check out Beau. He's bad news. I pushed for months for her to break it off with him."

"But I can't tell you for sure it was him," Euthelva said.

Alex nodded. "I understand."

"How did Charlotte die?" Euthelva whispered.

"We aren't sure yet," I said. "Doc Drago will need to confirm that."

"Hopefully we'll know by tomorrow." Alex stood. "I think that's all the questions we have right now. Again, we're sorry for your loss."

Nodding, Euthelva wrapped her arms around Annaleigh, and the two of them shuffled to the door.

"It's pretty late," I said when the door closed. "Do we talk to Beau tonight or in the morning?"

"In the morning. We have no idea where he is right now. It's a Friday night, and I doubt he's home. It sounds like time of death was between nine-twenty and nine-forty."

I nodded. "Makes sense."

"Let's say goodnight to Tommy."

I grinned and slipped my hand into his. "Good thing my fiancé can fly. We can be home in less than fifteen minutes."

He leaned down and brushed his lips against mine. "Is that why you're marrying me?"

"It's not the only reason…but it's a perk!"

7

"Tell me everything," Zoie demanded fifteen minutes later when Alex and I staggered wearily into the kitchen. She was perched on a barstool, sipping hot chocolate. "I've been waiting up so I can hear what happened."

"Yes, tell us everything." Needles sat precariously on the counter eating a pretzel. *"What did we miss? Who died?"*

"I'll tell you what's general knowledge," Alex said. "Charlotte Stoneman was killed sometime after her party tonight. Shayla found her body."

"I'm so sorry!" Zoie ran over and hugged me. "You must be gutted."

I smiled and patted her back. "I'm upset, but it's Serena who knew her best."

"Poor Serena. I should bake her something tomorrow to make her feel better."

"Speaking of," Alex said. "Shouldn't you be in bed? You have a busy day tomorrow."

Zoie grinned and waved her hand in the air. "Serena gave me

the day off from the bakery since it's prom. I can sleep all day, if I want."

Alex reached out and ran his hand down his daughter's back. "Well, Shayla and I need to be up early, so finish your hot chocolate."

"Just did before you came in."

"I may need more information to go on," Needles said. *"If this case is to get my full attention, I need all the facts."*

Alex rolled his eyes. "As the sheriff and lead investigator, I can assure you I have this handled. This doesn't really require your full attention."

"Blasphemy!" Needles shot up from the counter, his wings glowing red. *"Of course you need my help. I'm indispensable."*

Grinning, I snatched a pretzel from the bag on the counter. "Yeah, Alex. Don't you know Needles is indispensable?"

Needles narrowed his eyes at me. *"Do you jest, Princess?"*

I laughed and held up my hands in surrender. "Of course not."

Zoie frowned and put her hands behind her back. "Now that you have a case, Shayla, you won't be too busy to help me get ready for prom tomorrow night, will you?"

"Of course not."

"Promise?"

I reached out and pulled her to me, giving her a quick hug. "Of course, I promise. You are one of the most important things to me. I'll always make time for you."

She squeezed me back, then lifted a hand and used her magic to place the mug of cocoa in the sink. "C'mon, Needles. Let's go count some sheep."

Needles, wings shimmering green, zipped over to Zoie, and the two chatted amiably as they left the kitchen.

"I should go tell Dad what's happened," I said as I rinsed out

Zoie's glass. "But I'm too exhausted. We'll have to do it tomorrow."

Alex wrapped his arms around me and nuzzled my neck. "Tomorrow is good. I know you have to be physically and emotionally drained."

"You're right." Waving my hand in the air, I used my magic to turn off the lights. "Tomorrow's a new day. And a new mystery to solve."

* * *

"W*ho're we putting the screws to first?"* Needles asked from the backseat of Alex's Blazer.

"We aren't putting the screws to anyone," Alex said dryly.

"I think we need to question the ex-boyfriend, Beau," I said. "Then we should talk to Ellen Vampton. She made a scene at the party last night, *and* we know she was angry at Charlotte."

"Anyone else?" Alex asked.

I sighed. "We need to figure out what happened to Charlotte's necklace. If Doc didn't find it on Charlotte's body, then it could be the killer took it."

"How many people were at the party last night? Sixty?" Alex mused. "Because that's about how many suspects we now have."

I groaned and rested my head against the window. "I know. I don't even want to think about it."

My cell phone pinged, and I pulled it out of my pants pocket. Since it was Saturday, *and* I was officially off the clock for a few days, I didn't feel it necessary to wear my game warden uniform. I read the message, then shoved the phone back in my pocket.

"Serena says to stop by the bakery. She's already heard some gossip."

"Not surprising," Alex murmured.

"Thank the goddess," Needles said. *"I figured you'd just make me starve."*

I rolled my eyes. "When have I *ever* starved you?"

"I've forgotten, but that's not surprising. One of the first things to go when you're starving is your thought process. Soon I won't be able to string together a full sentence."

"If only we were that lucky," Alex muttered.

Twenty minutes later, Alex pulled to a stop along the curb outside Enchanted Bakery & Brew. It was packed—which wasn't unusual for a Saturday morning—but the customers today seemed more inclined to stand and gossip than to eat pastries.

We pushed our way to the counter where Serena and Tamara were busy filling orders and ringing up customers.

"Do you want me to call Zoie in?" I asked. "I know she wouldn't mind."

Serena waved her hand in dismissal. "Heavens, no. We can handle this."

"What can I get you?" Tamara asked.

Alex ordered a cinnamon roll, while I ordered an elderberry muffin for me and a caramel pretzel for Needles. The two large coffees were a given.

"So what's the big news?" I asked as Alex handed Serena cash. "What have you heard?"

Serena leaned forward so as not to be overheard. "Grant told me this morning as I left that Alex told him there might be a necklace missing from Charlotte's body. Well, I know who has it."

My eyes went wide. "What? Who?"

"Gretchen Clawman."

"How do you know?" I asked.

"I saw it with my own eyes. She was at the party last night, remember? Anyway, she came in this morning to get a cupcake, and when she heard the news, she got really upset and started crying. She pulled out a necklace from under her shirt and told me Charlotte gave her the necklace last night as Gretchen was leaving the party."

Needles snorted. *"That's convenient."*

"Do you know where Gretchen works?" I asked.

"She should be home," Serena said. "She picked up some cupcakes and said she was going home to cry and do some emotional eating."

I nodded. "Thanks, Serena. Let me know if you hear anything else."

"Be careful, and I'll see you at your place around four-thirty to get started on Zoie's hair."

Alex, Needles, and I pushed our way through the crowd once again and stepped outside.

"Guess our first stop should be Gretchen Clawman's place." I opened my passenger-side door to let Needles in. "More to cross her off the list. Could be what she said is true, and Charlotte gave her the necklace."

"Could be she's lying, and she's the killer, and I'll need to cut out her lying tongue."

I rolled my eyes and buckled my seatbelt as Alex pulled up Gretchen's address on his phone using the program IT forensic specialist, Gordon Hoots, had developed. It pinpointed every house on Enchanted Island.

"She's over on Lightning Lane," Alex said. "Looks like it's near the west side of town."

"Let's go see what Gretchen can tell us."

8

Lightning Lane was a cute subdivision made up of one-story cape cod houses. Cobblestone walkways lined most of the street, and Gretchen's tan with white and teal trim house was no different. Alex parked in her driveway, and the three of us headed for her front door.

"Do you know Gretchen?" Alex mused as he rapped on the door.

"Not really. She has an older sister who's a few years younger than me."

The front door opened, and a curvy, compact woman with shoulder-length brown hair, hazel eyes, and full lips stared out at us—in her left hand was a cupcake I recognized from Enchanted Bakery & Brew. She was dressed in lounge pants, a graphic t-shirt, and her bare feet sported metallic purple nail polish.

"Don't take this the wrong way," she said, "but this day just keeps getting worse and worse."

Needles landed on my shoulder. *"Best greeting I've had in years."*

"You might as well come in." She held up her pink and white cupcake. "As you can see, I'm eating my body weight in cupcakes today." Gretchen stepped back and motioned us inside with her head. "I'm also having coffee with lots of Irish cream. Want some?"

Alex smiled. "No, thanks. We just had coffee."

"Sans the Irish cream, unfortunately," I added.

Gretchen laughed. "Let's go to the kitchen. Does—Needles, right?"

I nodded.

"Does Needles need anything?"

"Pretzels, salt water, and a couple palm leaves fanning me would be great."

"He's fine," I said.

"Spoilsport." Needles flew from my shoulder and settled down on the top of a kitchen chair, his wings glowing green and yellow.

Gretchen, Alex, and I sat down around the table as well, and Gretchen shoved the bakery box toward us. "Take whatever you want." She took a huge bite of the cupcake she had in her hand, closed her eyes, and sighed as she chewed. Taking a huge gulp of her Irish coffee, she washed the cupcake down. "Better. Okay, I'm ready to be beaten with a rubber hose."

I let out a little bark of laughter. "We aren't here to beat you with a rubber hose, Gretchen."

"We aren't?" Needles mused. *"Then why're we here?"*

Doing my best to ignore Needles, I continued. "We're here to piece together everything that happened last night."

Tears filled Gretchen's eyes. "I just can't believe it. I saw you at the party last night. I didn't say hi or anything. But I saw you and Serena." She swiped at the tear that leaked from her eye with one hand, then clutched the necklace she had around her neck. “Charlotte gave this to me. That’s the last time I’ll ever see her.”

“Let’s start right there,” Alex said. “Why did Charlotte give you the necklace?”

“About two months ago, one of the magazines I freelance for went belly up, which meant no job for me. It was a big blow to my monthly income. I came into her shop and asked how much a necklace would be if it was charmed with the ability to give me peace and make me less anxious. She quoted me a price, and it was a little steep.” She waved her hand in the air. “I don’t exactly make a lot of money as a freelance writer. My parents moved to the mainland years ago, and my sister was already married and living on the south side of the island, so my parents let me stay here in my childhood home. Otherwise, I’d be living a lot differently, trust me.”

“I hear you.” Needles’ wings brushed my hair. *“I’ve been meaning to ask for a raise myself.”*

“Dream on,” I muttered. It wasn’t the first time Needles had mentioned getting a raise.

“What?” Gretchen asked.

“Nothing,” I said, ignoring Alex’s grin. “You were saying?”

“Oh, right. So when my anxiety didn’t get any better on its own, I went to see Charlotte again at her shop. I told her I had fifty bucks saved up, and was there anything she could make me at that price.” Gretchen picked up her cupcake, took another bite, and chewed. “She told me she had something in mind, and she’d give it to me next week. She then invited me to her party.” Gretchen shrugged. “I didn’t know her that well. I mean, she was ahead of me in school, and outside of visiting her shop on occasion, we didn’t exactly socialize.”

“But you went to the party anyway?” I mused.

“Yeah. She called me Thursday and said she’d give me the

necklace Friday night at her party—that is, if I was going to be attending. I told her absolutely, and I'd see her there."

"And when exactly did Charlotte give you the necklace?" I asked.

"It was near the end of the party. I'd say a good ten or twenty people had already left. I saw you and Serena still there. Anyway, she saw me, called me over, and we went outside for a minute to talk privately. She took the necklace off from around her neck and told me she made it for herself when her parents died. She'd been having nightmares back then, and it was the first piece she ever made. She said it would bring me peace when I needed it." Gretchen swallowed hard, trying to fight back the tears. "I was so touched. I mean, it was her first piece of jewelry she ever made and she was giving it to me."

"That *was* nice of her," I agreed. "Did you see anyone outside? Maybe someone lurking around the alley or back parking lot?"

Gretchen shook her head. "No. I've thought about it a ton of times since I heard the news." She wiped away a tear. "I feel so *guilty*!"

The last word came out on a wail as Gretchen plunked her head on the table and sobbed.

"Why do you feel guilty?" Alex asked.

Gretchen lifted her head, tears spilling down her cheeks. "Be—because if it wasn't fo—for me, Charlotte would still be *alive*."

"How so?" I asked.

"Don't you see?" Gretchen sat up straighter and wiped away her tears. "If Charlotte hadn't taken off the necklace and given it to me, she'd still be alive. She took it off and was no longer protected."

It wasn't exactly rational, but I could see why Gretchen

would feel that way. "Did you leave the party after she gave you the necklace?"

Gretchen nodded, grabbed another cupcake out of the box, and swiped a finger across the icing. "Yeah. I came home and went right to sleep." She stuck her finger with the icing in her mouth. "Woke up, felt like celebrating, so I got dressed and went to Enchanted Bakery & Brew to splurge on a cupcake or two. The bakery was already abuzz with the news Charlotte was dead, and when I heard, I just freaked out! I think I told Serena about the necklace while she boxed my cupcakes. It's a little bit of a blur." She set down her cupcake and wrapped her hands around her coffee cup. "Is that why you're here? You think I stole the necklace and killed Charlotte? I didn't. I swear!"

"We're just trying to talk with people who were at the party," Alex said, "and people who had direct contact with Charlotte. No one is saying you killed her."

"I liked her. I really did. I had no reason to kill her."

Alex nodded to me, and we stood from the table. "Thank you for speaking with us today, Gretchen." He glanced down at her cupcakes. "Enjoy your sweets."

She laughed shakily and rose. "Do you guys want one for the road?"

"No, thanks," I said.

"I'd like one or two." Needles zipped over to where Gretchen stood, his wings shimmering gold and silver. *"They never think of me. They practically starve me all day."*

"He's adorable," Gretchen said.

Needles sucked in a breath. *"Adorable? Hear me well, Werewolf. I am* not *adorable! I am a fierce warrior whose enemies quake in fear at the mere sight of me. A warrior so fierce, songs have been written about me!"*

"Oh, brother," Alex muttered.

"Would your little friend like a treat?" Gretchen asked.

Needles did a somersault in the air, his wings glowing green and yellow. *"You're too kind. I'd* love *a cupcake."*

"No, thanks," I said. "Sugar gives Needles gas."

"You are dead to me, Princess."

Gretchen giggled and walked us to the door.

"I don't think she's a suspect," Alex said when we got back inside his Blazer.

"I agree. She didn't know Charlotte well, so there was no motive to kill her. But at least now we know the killer didn't steal the necklace."

"One case solved," Needles said. *"Who are we grilling next?"*

"Beau," I said. "Let's go see what the ex has to say."

9

Up close, Beau Broombotten was an intimidating-looking man. He had shoulder-length black hair, piercing dark eyes, and a thin, sharp face. He'd opened his front door in nothing but low-rise jeans—so low it was almost criminal. His chest and arms were covered in tattoos, and it was obvious from his huge yawn and scowl our pounding had roused him out of bed.

"Whatcha want?" he demanded, taking in Alex's uniform. "I was home by one-thirty, so if whatever you're here about happened after that time, I didn't do it."

"Mind if we come in?" Alex asked.

Beau scratched his chest, looked from Alex, to me, to Needles…then shrugged. "Suit yourself."

He ambled farther inside the dark and dingy apartment. Picking up a bottle of beer off the coffee table, he took a swig.

"That's the most vile thing I've seen in a long time," Needles said. *"It's probably a good thing you didn't feed me that cupcake because it would be coming back up right about now."*

"May we sit?" Alex asked.

I wanted to say no, we should stand, but I didn't want to make Beau even more defensive. Perched gingerly on the edge of the orange and black plaid couch, I glanced around the room, taking in the guitars and potion bottles. A unique combination, for sure.

"Do you know why we're here, Mr. Broombotten?" Alex asked.

"Nope. Not a clue." He leaned back in his chair and looked at me. "Do I know you?"

"I don't think so. My name is Shayla Loci, and I'm the game warden for Enchanted Island."

"A chick game warden. That's cool." He scratched his armpit. "Explains the flying rodent. Not sure why a game warden is here, but whatever."

"Flying rodent!" Needles whipped out two quills from his back and charged Beau.

Beau held up a hand. "Whoa! Little dude. Step back."

But Needles wasn't having it. He whipped his quills across Beau's palm, causing the witch to curse under his breath and shake his hand back and forth.

"Crap! That hurts! I'm freakin' bleeding, man."

Alex and I sat calmly by, waiting for the theatrics to end.

"Gonna hurt even more when I carve out your tongue, roast it over a spit, and make you eat it!"

"It's typically not a good idea to disrespect my partner," I said. "Needles doesn't take kindly to it."

Beau held up his other hand—the one *not* bleeding—his eyes wide. "Sure. Sure. Whatever, man. No offense."

Needles continued to stare at Beau, his red wings fluttering rapidly. Finally, with one last look over his shoulder, Needles flew back to me and settled onto my shoulder.

"He should come with a warning sign," Beau muttered.

"Do you know Charlotte Stoneman?" Alex asked.

Beau snorted and rolled his eyes. "C'mon. Don't tell me that lame family of hers called you to harass me?"

"Not exactly," Alex said.

When Alex didn't say anything else, Beau shrugged. "Yeah, I know her. I dated that stiff-lip Charlotte for a while. Why?"

"Did you go to the party for her last night?" Alex asked.

"Yep. And can you believe they asked me to leave?" He grinned. "That family has no sense of humor."

"They had name tags at the door," I said. "Did you get one?"

Beau frowned. "I guess. Why?"

"Do you still have it?" I asked, ignoring his question.

"No. When that gorilla of a troll threw me out, I tore it off and threw it at her."

"Charming. I say you give me five minutes alone with him."

"You tore it off and threw it at Lucia?" I repeated.

Hearing the contempt in my voice, Beau flushed. "Yeah. Pissed me off."

I gestured to his potions along one wall. "You practice?"

"Sure do. Between gigs."

"Gigs?" I mused. "You're a musician?"

"Musician and bartender. My band and I play mostly at Bites & Beer, a vampire bar, but sometimes we play at Wolfsbane. It's a little edgier than Bites & Beer."

I stood and strolled over to his shelves of potions. "You got a nice collection here."

He shrugged. "I've always made my own. Got something for just about anything that ails you."

"What about spells? You pretty good at those?" I asked, returning to the couch.

"Yeah, I guess. Why? What's all this about?"

"What do you know about death spells?" Alex asked.

Beau snorted. "Uh, they cause death. Duh." He grinned. "When used correctly, they work well."

"Can you do a death spell?" I asked.

"Why? You got someone you need rid of?" He ran his eyes over me. "I'd think you could do that on your own. You radiate something I can't place. Something powerful and—well, almost scary."

Good. I wanted him to fear me.

"Black Forest King will be pleased you can make your enemies quake, Princess."

"I don't do dark magic," I said stiffly. "What about you?"

Beau shrugged. "Maybe. It ain't illegal. You gonna tell me why you're all here asking me annoying questions so early in the morning?"

"It's ten-thirty," Alex said dryly.

"Exactly, dude. I should be in bed."

"Do you know how to do a death spell?" I asked again, this time with a little more force.

"All right. Jeez. Yeah, I guess I could look it up in one of my books."

"What time did you leave the party last night?" I asked.

"I told you already. After that troll threw me out, I left."

"You didn't stand around in the parking lot? Maybe wait and see if Charlotte would come out after the party?"

Beau narrowed his eyes. "Okay, maybe. Maybe I did. No crime in that." He shrugged. "Didn't see her though."

Alex sat forward on the couch. "You're saying you didn't accost Charlotte after the party, perform a death spell on her, and then leave her body behind the dumpster?"

Beau's mouth fell open, and his eyes went wide. "What? Are

you saying Charlotte's dead?" He ran his hands over his face. "Whoa. This is crazy, man. Absolutely crazy."

"So you didn't know?" I asked.

"How the heck would I know? I've been sleeping."

"You were pretty angry at Charlotte when she broke up with you," I said. "Lots of people have testified to that."

"So what? I got over it."

"Really?" I mused. "Is that why you felt the need to stop by the party last night? Because you were over Charlotte and not upset she was leaving the island?"

A muscle jumped in Beau's jaw, and I could tell I hit a nerve.

"Score one for you, Princess."

Beau shrugged. "So? Maybe I was a little mad she was leaving. Doesn't mean I killed her."

"You admitted you were in the back parking lot waiting for her to leave the party," I said. "Did you see her?"

"No. I waited in the back, sure. But when that battle ax, Euthelva, came out to her car with a box and saw me, she got all squinty-eyed and looked like she was going to hex me. So I got out of there."

"Where did you go after that?" I asked.

"I went and hung out at Bites & Beer."

"What time would that be?" I asked.

"I don't know. It's not like I kept track of my time last night. Like I said, I'm pretty sure I was home by one-thirty." He snapped his fingers. "Hey, you wanna talk to someone who hated her? Talk to Ellen Vampton. I went by Charlotte's shop last week, and man—"

"Why?" I demanded. "Why did you go by Charlotte's store?"

Beau gave me an oily grin. "It's a free country. I can go wherever I want."

"What about Ellen?" Alex mused. "What did you see?"

Beau stared at me a minute longer before turning his attention to Alex. "I was in the store when Ellen Vampton came in. Everyone knows about her problem with her husband, so I wasn't surprised to see her there. She starts yelling at Charlotte how none of her charms are working. She'd bought every stone Charlotte had suggested and still nothing." Beau snorted. "Ellen was pretty pissed. Demanding all her money back. Said if Charlotte didn't refund her money for all the purchases she'd made over the last six months, that Charlotte would regret it."

"And what did Charlotte say?" I asked.

Beau shrugged. "Not much. Asked her to calm down, and then she took her to the back room."

Alex stood. "We'll be checking your alibi, Beau."

Beau shrugged. "Whatever, man."

10

Ellen Vampton lived on the northwest side of the island, about fifteen minutes from town, and five miles inland from the water. That area of the island was heavily populated with vampires, while the selkies and mermaids typically lived closer to the coast.

Like a lot of the homes in that area of the island, they were more manors and estates than houses. When Alex turned onto the private lane that would take us to the Vampton home, I let out a whistle when I saw the house in the distance.

"What do the Vamptons do for a living?" I mused.

Alex chuckled. "It always makes me laugh when you say stuff like that after seeing other people's homes. You live in a *castle,* Shayla."

I grinned. "Yeah, but a castle built by my dad."

"I'm not sure what they do for a living. Guess we'll have to ask that question."

The two-story stone structure was at least four thousand square feet, with ornate stained glass windows dominating the façade. The perfectly landscaped yard—at least ten acres—had to be professionally maintained. Otherwise, either Mr. or Mrs. Vampton would spend all their waking hours outside.

Alex pulled into the circle drive and parked next to a large fountain. "Okay, I'll give it to you. It's a nice place."

When we were out of the vehicle, Needles zipped over to the water fountain, his wings glowing blue and silver, and poked out his tongue to catch some of the dripping water. *"You need to put one of these inside the castle, Princess."*

"And have you getting water all over the floor? Pass."

The front door opened before we even knocked, and a sour-faced lady in a traditional maid's uniform stared out at us. "This is the Vampton residence. How may I help you?"

"I'm Sheriff Stone, and these are my associates Shayla Loci and Needles. We'd like to speak to Ellen Vampton."

"Is Mrs. Vampton expecting you?"

"No," Alex said. "But I'm sure if you let her know we're here, she will see us."

"Please stay here while I inquire if Mrs. Vampton is taking visitors today."

Alex tapped the badge on his chest. "Remind her it's the sheriff."

The woman nodded once and firmly shut the door.

"I also say we get one of those," Needles said. *"I'm tired of constantly having to open the door in the Castle."*

I scoffed and rolled my eyes. "First of all, you always elect to open the door. And second, we rarely have visitors that need to knock."

Before Needles could argue, the front door opened again and the stoic woman gestured us inside.

"Please follow me. Mrs. Vampton will see you in the parlor. I am to inquire if you would like anything to drink."

"No, thank you," Alex said

I glanced over at Needles, surprised he hadn't argued. But he was too enthralled with all the statues and gemstones and geodes dominating the foyer.

We followed the housekeeper down a wide carpeted hallway. When we reached an arched doorway on the left, she motioned us inside before walking away.

"She's not exactly a talker, is she?" Needles snickered.

Ellen Vampton sat on a buttery yellow chaise with a book on her lap. When we entered, she closed the book and set it on the table beside her.

"I suppose you are here to see me about what happened to Charlotte. Well, you might as well come in and sit down." She motioned for us to sit on the pale blue sofa across from her. "I'm not sure what all I can tell you. I wasn't at the party long."

"So you know Charlotte is dead?" Alex asked.

"Yes. I've had friends ringing me all morning."

I glanced around the room and took in the copious number of stones and gems—rose quartz, aventurine, citrine, aquamarine, fluorite, jade, and moonstone. And those were just the ones I could identify.

"This is an amazing collection you have." I gestured around the room. "I know enough to know they all have one thing in common."

Ellen narrowed her eyes. "It's no secret I was angry at Charlotte. She bilked me out of thousands of dollars." She reached over and picked up rose quartz off the table. "I surrounded myself with these stones and statues, and I doused myself in every piece of jewelry she made me. And it still did no good." She set the rose quartz back down. "None of it did any good."

"You and your husband cannot conceive?" I asked.

Ellen closed her eyes briefly. "We cannot. We've been seriously trying for about a year now, and that charlatan Charlotte said she could help me."

"How long have you been buying from Charlotte?" I asked.

"At least eight months. Maybe longer."

I frowned. "Why the sudden urge to confront her last night? Was it because she was leaving the island?"

Ellen dropped her legs onto the floor and sat up. "Not that it's any of your business, but Charlotte refused to sell me any more pieces. She said she had done everything she could for me. When I pressed her on it, she called my husband and told him she could not in good conscience sell me any more jewelry. Well, he had no idea what she was talking about, and when she told him, he was livid. He had no idea how much I'd spent on the jewelry and all these stones, much less what it was for." She leaped up from the chaise and started to pace. "Now suddenly he takes an interest in what I'm doing? I'm not sure who I'm angrier with…him or Charlotte."

"Well, seeing as how Charlotte is dead, I'd say Charlotte." Needles popped out from under my hair and dropped to perch on the armrest next to me.

"Is that an animal?" Ellen stopped pacing and stared at Needles. "I don't allow animals in my house. Filthy things."

Needles shot up from the armrest, his wings glowing bright red. *"Filthy? Oh, that's rich. I can smell you stinking supernaturals a mile away."*

I was about to snatch Needles out of the air when Ellen gasped. "Your wings are the same color as the carnelian stone. One of the most popular fertility stones around. I wonder if it would work if I took one of your wings and put it under our bed?"

You could've heard a pin drop. The only sound in the room was the buzzing of Needles' wings as they fluttered rapidly. I'm not sure who was most startled by her declaration—me, Alex, or Needles.

Needles slowly reached behind him and plucked two quills from his back. *"Try it, you crazy witch, and it'll be the last thing you do."*

"If you're willing to kill an animal because its coloring matches that of a fertility stone," I mused. "I have to wonder how easy it would be for you to kill another supernatural?"

Ellen scoffed and sat back down on the chaise, still staring at Needles. "I didn't kill Charlotte Stoneman." She finally drew her eyes from Needles and reclined into the chaise lounge. "But I'm also not the least bit sad she's dead."

"So you admit to being at the party last night?" Alex mused.

"Of course. It would be foolish for me to deny it. I'm sure dozens of people saw me there."

"Did you put on one of those name tags at the door?" I asked.

Ellen waved her hand in the air. "Yes. Stupidest thing ever. When I went to take it off, it stuck to my shirt. Took me three tries to get it completely ripped off. I should probably send that spineless cousin, Annaleigh, the dry cleaning bill."

"Annaleigh doesn't strike me as spineless," I mused.

Ellen scoffed. "Please, she's a Normal. A family full of witches, and she can't even do a simple spell. Instead, she has to rely on magic from others around here. Spineless and useless."

It might have been wrong of me, but I was suddenly glad this woman couldn't have children. It was one thing to hate animals, but I had to wonder how she would react if her own child turned out to be a Normal. Could she love him or her unconditionally? Or would she tell the child it, too, was spineless and useless?

"What did you do after you left the party?" Alex asked, when I continued to just stare in amazement at Ellen.

"I got in my car, and I drove to Bites & Beer."

I frowned. "That place doesn't strike me as your cup of tea."

"It's not. But I wanted to see my husband."

"He hangs out there?" I asked.

Ellen let out a bark of laughter. "Not to socialize, dear. Henry *owns* the bar."

11

I placed a to-go order at the Enchanted Island Café as Alex drove us back to town. Seconds later, I received a text from Serena. Reading it, I laughed out loud.

"Seems Zoie texted Serena she was nervous about tonight and asked Serena to bring home every extra chocolate pastry available."

Alex smiled. "Sounds like Zoie."

"And caramel pretzels," Needles said from the backseat. *"I'm nervous as well."*

I scoffed. "Why're you nervous?"

"Do you know how long it's been since I had to sharpen my quills in front of a boy to intimidate him?"

"I remember you doing that to me not long ago," Alex said dryly.

"Oh, right." Needles chuckled. *"Forgot about that, Gargoyle. I mean besides that time."*

Alex pulled to a stop in front of the café, and I ran in to get the food. I'd ordered an extra soup and sandwich combo for

Grant. I figured he and Opal had already eaten, but Grant was a werewolf—his metabolism made it so he constantly had to consume calories. No way would it go to waste.

As I climbed back inside the Blazer, Alex disconnected his cell. "That was Doc. He's ready to see us."

"I'll fly your food upstairs for you," Needles said. *"This way, you guys can go down to the dead doctor's lab without me."*

Nothing Needles hated more than dead bodies. Which was funny, seeing as how he was once the fiercest and deadliest warrior—or so he liked to say.

When we got to the station and stepped inside the building, I handed Needles the bag. He zipped over to the sheriff's station while Alex and I headed downstairs to the forensic area.

Octogenarian Pearl Earthly-Caraway was guarding the front office as usual. Her twin sister, Opal, worked behind the desk upstairs in the sheriff's department. When we hit the bottom of the stairs, Pearl looked up and gave us a gap-tooth smile.

"Well, well. If it isn't the gargoyle and the witch. How're the wedding plans coming along? You need my help with the bachelorette party?"

I suppressed a shudder. No way did I need her or her sister's help. The twins had recently gotten married for the first time to twin witch brothers, and I'd nearly fallen out of my chair when the sisters announced they were having male strippers at their bachelorette party.

"I'm sure Serena can handle the party planning," I said. "But thanks for the offer."

"What about the honeymoon? You got that covered yet?"

I shook my head and elbowed Alex in the side, hoping he'd step in...but he just kept his mouth shut. I shot him a death glare before turning back to Pearl. "Not yet. Listen, Pearl, we really need to see Doc."

Pearl harrumphed. "You young people, always in a hurry. Well, I suppose you're here to see him about the autopsy." Ever so slowly, Pearl reached for her phone and hit a button. "Doc, the sheriff and game warden are here to see you. They seem to be in quite a hurry." She paused. "Will do." She slowly placed the receiver back in the cradle. "Doc says you can go on back. Don't forget, if you need help planning anything, Opal and I are your girls."

Girls was a bit of a stretch, but I just smiled and nodded as I hurried after Alex.

"Please don't let them plan anything," Alex murmured.

I grinned. "Didn't even cross my mind."

Alex knocked on Doc's laboratory door and pushed it open. Both Doc and Finn were standing near his computer, looking at the screen.

"Hey, Doc. Finn." I sent her a small wave. "Whaddya got for us?"

Doc motioned us over to the body under the sheet on his table. Pulling the cover down, he exposed Charlotte's face and upper torso. "You were right, Shayla. It was a death curse. It was like her larynx had been crushed from the inside. She was healthy for her age, and her other organs all looked good. I found alcohol in her system, along with chocolate cake and what I assumed might be finger foods from the party. No illegal or prescription drugs of any kind."

"How long would it have taken her to die?" Alex asked.

"I can't be certain," Doc said. "I don't know much about death spells."

"No more than fifteen seconds," I murmured. "It would have been quick, but painful."

"I didn't find anything surprising from the torn name tag," Finn said. "There *was* a fingerprint, but it came back belonging to Charlotte. She was already in the Enchanted Island database."

"I scraped under her nails," Doc said, "but they were clean. No apparent struggle, except for when she grabbed the name tag and ripped it off. But it must have been a clean tear because there weren't any fibers present."

"Not a lot for us to go on," Alex said.

Doc nodded. "Yes, I'm afraid all I could do was confirm it was a death spell. Haven't seen one of those in a while."

"Okay," Alex said. "If you find something you think we need to know about, just text. Shayla and I are going to be upstairs going over everything with Grant."

"Is Zoie ready for tonight?" Finn asked.

I grinned. "Well, she sent a text about half an hour ago saying she was nervous and needed chocolate."

Finn threw back her head and laughed. "Oh, I remember those nights. Good for her. I'm sure she and Brick will have a fabulous time."

We said goodbye and headed back upstairs. Pearl was on the phone giggling and paying us no attention. I figured she was talking to her new husband and just kept walking.

When Alex opened the door to the sheriff's station, Opal called out a greeting. "Hello, Shayla. Sheriff. Grant and Needles are in the lounge."

Calling the cramped enclosure a lounge was a bit of a stretch. It had a sink, mini fridge, microwave, and a four-person table. When we walked inside, Grant motioned to the bag on the table.

"I kept it covered and warm for you guys." He took a huge bite of the sandwich, chewed, then swallowed. "Thanks for thinking of me."

I reached out and started to unpack the rest of the food. "I figured you wouldn't say no."

"I have to be careful, though," Grant said. "This second trimester has Serena crazy with the cravings, and I find myself eating right along with her."

Alex chuckled and took a bite of his sandwich. "You worried about putting on a little extra weight?"

Grant patted his flat stomach. "A little. Probably gonna need to squeeze in a few extra night runs with Dash."

"Want to wait until we finish eating before we go over suspects and motives?" I asked. "Or do it now?"

"I can do two things at once." Grant picked up the paper sitting on the table. "Got backgrounds right here."

"Who's first on the list?" Alex asked.

"Beau Broombotten. Multiple arrests and charges, and all in the supernatural courts. There are a couple that have to do with assault."

"Any significant jail time?" I asked.

"Did a year in another supernatural jailhouse on the mainland," Grant said. "Other than that, just a couple months here and there."

"Motive?" Alex mused.

"He was angry when he came to the party last night," I said. "Was enraged Charlotte was leaving the island for another man, and we know he's been stalking her for nearly a year now."

"Jealousy is always an excellent motive to kill," Grant said.

I nodded. "True enough. He's also a witch who admits he can do a death spell. We know he had on a name tag at the party, and he was seen by Euthelva standing outside the building later that night around the time Charlotte was killed."

"Shayla and I still need to check his alibi," Alex said. "He claims he left immediately after Euthelva saw him and went to Bites & Beer. It takes about fifteen minutes to get there from town, so depending on what time he arrived will depend on whether or not he's still in the window as a possible suspect."

"And the window is?" Grant asked.

"Between nine-twenty and nine-forty," I said. "Best we can tell."

"Next, we have Annaleigh Hexly. Background on her shows she was arrested when she was twenty in another supernatural town on the mainland. The report I got back from their court said aggravated assault, which was pleaded down to simple assault. The sentence was deferred, and she received a year probation."

"Well, we know she can't do magic," Alex said. "So how could she have done the spell? That seems to be my biggest question regarding Annaleigh being a suspect."

I scraped up the last of my soup, then set the spoon down. "It's not ideal, but she could have gotten the death spell off the dark supernatural Internet. Typically, the spell is done face-to-face, but in this case, if Annaleigh is our killer, then she may have gotten the spell as a potion. She would only have a certain amount of time to invoke the spell, so it had to have been done at the party."

"Could she have dumped the potion in one of Charlotte's drinks?" Alex asked.

I nodded. "Yes. From there, all Annaleigh had to do was wait for a time they were alone in the parking lot, say the words the maker of the spell gave Annaleigh, and it would have the same effect as if Annaleigh could wield magic." I unwrapped my sandwich and flattened the paper. "I saw Annaleigh hand Charlotte at least two drinks last night, so it's plausible." I closed my eyes and pulled up an image of Annaleigh sitting in Tommy's office after the murder. "You know, I don't think I remember Annaleigh having on her name tag in Tommy's office while we were talking to her and her mom. Do you remember seeing Annaleigh's name tag, Alex?"

Alex shook his head. "No, but I don't recall Euthelva having one either. They *did* go home and come back to the party when they heard about Charlotte. Maybe they'd already taken them off."

"That's true." I took a small bite of my grilled cheese sandwich and moaned at the deliciousness. "We know Annaleigh has motive. Charlotte planned on selling the building she owned that housed their business to someone else. Also, with Charlotte leaving the island, Annaleigh no longer had a job. Granted, she can still make jewelry, but she can't infuse the stones and gems with magic. Charlotte basically stripped Annaleigh of a profitable income and a place to sell her jewelry."

"As far as I'm concerned," Alex said, "that's one of the strongest motives we have."

I nodded. "Plus, there's also a little jealousy. When I saw Annaleigh at Iris' flower shop Friday afternoon, she admitted to me she wished she could find someone like Charlotte had. She, too, was ready to settle down and start a family."

Grant pushed his chair back from the table and brushed crumbs from his hands. "Next, I have Euthelva Hexly. Mother to Annaleigh. No criminal record I could find."

"Well, we know she can do magic," I said. "Plus, she seemed a little put out with Charlotte leaving, and she wasn't happy Charlotte was selling the building to someone else."

"Last name you gave me was Ellen Vampton. No major criminal history. There are some hits for speeding here on the island, but that's about it."

"She's a witch married to a vampire," I said. "She can do magic, and she was livid at Charlotte. She blamed Charlotte for not being able to get pregnant, *and* she was mad Charlotte had told the husband, Henry, she wouldn't be selling Ellen anymore spelled baubles."

Grant whistled. "That's a big red flag for me. Typically, I never really paid attention to that kind of stuff, but now that Serena is pregnant, I can't tell you how attuned I am to others' emotions. Some people are genuinely happy for us, but there have been a few times when I could sense jealousy and envy."

I nodded. "I believe it. My impression was Ellen would do whatever it takes to have a baby. Heck, she even threatened to pull off one of Needles' wings because it looked like a certain fertility stone."

Needles looked up from the slab of salty ham he'd been quietly nibbling on for the last ten minutes, his wings glowing red and black. *"I should have cut off one of her fingers just for thinking it."*

"Are you serious?" Grant asked. "She really wanted to cut off one of Needles' wings?"

"Yeah," Alex said. "She's definitely obsessed. Her house was filled with fertility statues and all kinds of rocks and stones."

I took a drink of the bottled water Grant had set out before we arrived. "Ellen also claims to have left the party and went to Bites & Beer afterward. So that means both Ellen and Beau high-tailed it up to the northwest side of the island after the party."

"Do Ellen and Beau know each other?" Grant asked.

I shrugged. "I'm not sure, but I'd say yes. We definitely have more questions to ask regarding their relationship, but Beau told us his band sometimes plays at Bites & Beer, and he occasionally will bartend there. I'd say there's no way he and Ellen *can't* know each other."

"What about Gretchen Clawson?" Alex mused. "Can we cross her off on the list? I don't really see her as a suspect anymore. We know why she had Charlotte's necklace."

"I agree." I wiped my mouth with a napkin. "Her reasoning for having Charlotte's necklace rang true for me. And she doesn't really have any other motive to want Charlotte dead."

"Anyone else on the suspect list?" Grant asked.

I shook my head. "No, but I think we need to talk to Grey Wolfstein at some point. He's supposedly the one buying Charlotte's building."

"Which brings up another big question," Alex said. "With Charlotte dead, what happens to the building?"

"That's true," I said. "It could be Charlotte had something different in a will she hadn't changed yet."

Alex grinned. "I was thinking the same thing. Have you been able to reach the boyfriend, Grant?"

"I have. His name is James Jadeton, and he's flying to the island tomorrow."

"Good," Alex said. "I'd like to hear his take on everything."

I stuffed the last of the grilled cheese in my mouth and washed it down with the bottled water. "Ready to get back to work?"

"Just to keep you up to speed with things on my end," Grant said. "I spoke with Lester at Brooms Away. He said he never received a call from Charlotte for a pick up."

Alex nodded. "Okay, thanks for checking."

"Also, I finished the paperwork this morning regarding the land dispute on the east side of the island between the selkie and the werewolf." He glanced at his watch. "If it's okay with you, Alex, I'll knock off now. Serena should be done at the bakery and ready to go home for a quick nap before heading to the castle to help with Zoie."

"Sounds good," Alex said. "Shayla and I still need to talk with Grey Wolfstein and Lucia Trollski. If we get a good lead, we'll let you know."

12

Grey Wolfstein and his son were closing down their shop when Alex and I strolled inside. Needles had passed out in the backseat of the Blazer, so that's where we left him.

"Welcome," Grey called out. "I'd tell you to look around and let us know if you need help, but something tells me this isn't a visit to look for appliances."

Enchanted Appliances Plus was the only appliance store on the island as far as I knew, and Grey sold everything from new or used and enchanted or non-enchanted. For bakers and cooks like Serena, who had no need for an enchanted appliance, they could still get their needs met by buying non-enchanted. But for people like me, who could wield magic yet somehow couldn't manage a simple meal, this store was a godsend. The store also came in handy for Normals or other supernaturals who couldn't perform magic.

"I'm afraid this isn't a social visit," Alex said. "We need to talk to you about Charlotte Stoneman's death."

"Do you need me to stay as well?" Grey's son asked.

Alex shook his head. “I don’t believe so.”

“I should get home to Gracie, then.” He clapped his hand on Grey’s shoulder. “See you in the morning, Dad.”

Grey nodded, watched his son exit behind a door at the back of the store, then shuffled out from behind the counter. “Such a shame. She was a beautiful spirit that Charlotte. Helpful and generous.”

“We’ve heard you were supposed to buy her building,” I said.

“Sure was. Still hoping to. Just not sure what’s gonna happen now, though.”

“Were you surprised when Charlotte offered to sell to you?” I asked.

Grey nodded. “Oh, yes. I approached her first, you see. About two weeks ago, when I heard she was leaving. I figured she’d turn me down, but instead, she said she needed some time to think about it. Then a few days back—I think it was Monday—she came over and said she’d like to sell to me.”

“But you have no idea what will happen now?” I asked.

Grey clucked his tongue. “Sure don’t. But, I figure if the building goes to Annaleigh, maybe she’d be willing to sell to me.”

Alex leaned against an oven, then jolted when it came to life and asked what needed to be made. “Sorry.” He stepped back from the range and shoved his hands in his pockets. “Had you heard or seen anyone threaten Charlotte recently?”

“Can’t say as I have. I know she’s had some problems with that ex-boyfriend of hers, and I once had to run him off a few months back when I caught him hanging out behind her alley. But other than that, I can’t recall anything recent.”

Alex nodded. “What about her relationship with Annaleigh?”

“Oh, they’re very close. Almost like sisters.”

“So,” Alex mused, “you never heard any fighting or anything

like that?"

Grey's eyebrows shot up. "Goodness, no. They got along well, from what I could tell."

"Thank you for your time," Alex said. "I think that's all we have."

"I sure hope you catch who did this to that poor girl. Such a shame."

* * *

"What did we learn?" Alex mused as he turned onto Lucia Trollski's street.

"That as far as Grey knew, Annaleigh and Charlotte weren't having issues."

Alex nodded. "Exactly what I was thinking."

"So we concentrate more on Beau and Ellen?"

"Perhaps. Especially since Grey told us Beau was still hanging out around the store. We'll know more when we hear what Lucia has to say."

There were already two vehicles in Lucia's driveway, so Alex parked in front of her house. I could hear a lawnmower close by as I opened my door.

"You coming?" I asked Needles.

Needles zipped out of the vehicle, his green wings fluttering quickly. *"Of course. Unless you're* trying *to suffocate me by keeping me imprisoned inside the vehicle?"*

I rolled my eyes and strode up the walkway to the front porch, stepping over the myriad toys and bikes along the way.

Alex knocked on the door as Needles dropped to my shoulder, and a few seconds later it was opened by a tall, harried-looking woman with red eyes, a puffy face, and a chubby baby on her hip.

"Hi, Lucia," I said.

Lucia's eyes filled with tears. "I just can't believe this. I can't seem to stop crying. Who would do something like this?"

The little girl smacked her tiny hand against Lucia's face. "Mommy? Mommy?"

"Mommy's okay. She's just sad."

"Sad." The skinny ponytail on top of the child's head bobbed. "Mommy sad."

Smiling softly at her daughter, Lucia stepped back from the door. "Come in. My husband has the other two kids out in the backyard, keeping them distracted for me." She shifted the baby higher and crossed through the living room and into the kitchen. "Can I get you something to drink?"

"Drink!" the baby echoed.

"Yes, you can have a drink, Lexi." Lucia grabbed a sippy cup from the counter and handed it to her daughter. "Do you want to go outside and play with your brothers?"

Lexi plopped down on her diapered butt. "Stay. Drink."

Lucia smiled down at her daughter. "Okay. You can stay and drink while the grown-ups talk." She looked back up at us. "You're sure I can't get you something to drink?"

I shook my head. "We just had something not too long ago. We promise not to take up too much of your time."

Sighing, Lucia dropped down onto a kitchen chair. "I turned off my phone when I got home last night, so I didn't hear about Charlotte's death until this morning." A tear slipped down her cheek. "How did she die? The rumor going around was she was murdered."

"Death spell," I whispered.

Lucia gasped. "A death spell? But that's—well, that's not even supposed to be practiced anymore, I thought."

"It's not," I said.

Lexi, already bored, tossed her cup aside and wobbled to her feet. "Play."

Needles popped out from under my hair, his wings throwing off a kaleidoscope of colors. *"I got this covered, Princess."*

"Pretty! Pretty!"

Needles slowly flew to the other side of the kitchen, the little girl racing behind him, arms outstretched, and babbling in a language no one knew.

Lucia chuckled. "Is he available for babysitting?"

"Trust me, your kids would never be the same." I grinned. "In a good way."

Lucia laughed harder, wiping the tears from her cheeks. "Thanks. I needed that laugh. It's been a long day."

"And we won't keep you," Alex said. "We just need to ask you some questions about what happened last night at the party."

"I understand."

"There were at least two party crashers last night, right?" I asked.

Lucia nodded. "Yes. Both Ellen Vampton and Beau Broombotten showed up."

"And you threw them out?" Alex asked.

"I threw out Ellen, but Euthelva took care of Beau."

Alex nodded. "Okay. Did Ellen give you any trouble when you threw her out?"

Lucia shook her head. "Not really. She got a little lippy and tried to intimidate me by reminding me of who she was and who her husband was, but that's all." She rolled her eyes. "Like I care her vampire husband owns a bar." She waved her hand in the air. "I got three small kids. Who has time for bars anymore?"

"And Beau?" I mused. "Did you see what happened there?"

Lucia scoffed. "Beau. What a piece of work. I have no idea what Charlotte ever saw in him." Her eyes filled with tears again, and she took a gulp of whatever was in the travel mug in front of her. "Beau made some halfhearted threats to Euthelva, but nothing serious. She tossed him out, then shut the door in his face. I don't know where he went from there."

"You helped clean up, right?" I asked.

Lucia nodded. "Yeah, I carried a bunch of boxes out to the cars when needed." Her breath caught on a sob. "I also took out the trash. I can't help but play that over and over in my mind. Had Charlotte already been murdered and dumped just a few feet from where I was?"

"I'm sorry, Lucia," I said. "I know this must be hard. Did you ever see anyone in the alley on your trips to the cars?"

"I don't think so. At least, I didn't actually *see* anyone. I do remember before we were finished, I overheard Euthelva in the back lot yelling at someone."

I surreptitiously glanced at Alex. "But you didn't see who it was?"

Lucia shook her head. "No, sorry. I went back inside and helped a couple others move tables around while Euthelva and Annaleigh finished loading Euthelva's car."

I nodded. "Right. I remember the tables getting moved while I finished vacuuming. You say Charlotte was gone by then?"

Lucia nodded. "I'm pretty sure."

"We have to ask," I said. "Did you know of any problems between Charlotte and Annaleigh?"

Lucia closed her eyes briefly. "You're talking about Charlotte selling her business, right?" Lucia sighed. "I know it hurt Annaleigh's feelings. She was already struggling because Charlotte was leaving, and then for Charlotte to sell the business—or I guess the building. It was a blow. But I'm telling you, Annaleigh did *not* kill Charlotte. There's no way."

An ear-splitting squeal filled the kitchen as Lexi hopped up and down on her tiny legs, trying to snatch Needles out of the air.

"Any time now, Princess."

I bit back a smile. "Thanks, Lucia. This actually helps."

"Really?" She took another sip from her travel mug. "I'm supposed to go over to Euthelva's and Annaleigh's tonight to help with funeral arrangements." She dropped her head into her hands. "I just don't know if I'm up to it."

"I'm sure they'd understand if you begged off," I said.

Needles zipped back over to my shoulder, causing Lexi to again squeal and hobble after him.

Lucia stood and swooped Lexi up in her arms. "Is that all? I'd like to go be with my husband and kids right now."

Alex and I both stood as well.

"Of course," I said. "I'm really sorry for your loss. Serena told me how close you, Charlotte, and Annaleigh were."

"Thank you."

"We can show ourselves out," I said. "You go be with your family."

The three of us headed for the front door.

"Bye-bye, fly!" Lexi cried from the kitchen. "Bye-bye, fly."

Alex snickered as we stepped outside and strode to the Blazer. "She thinks you're a pesky fly. Imagine that?"

"Haha, Gargoyle."

"You know what this means?" I shut the passenger-side door. "Beau definitely fits into the timeline of possible suspects. Both Euthelva and Lucia believe they saw him in the back parking lot around the time Charlotte was killed."

"We should do a stakeout," Needles said.

"First things first," I said, clicking my seatbelt. "Let's get back to the castle so I can help Zoie get ready for prom."

13

"I'm almost finished." Serena wrapped the last of Zoie's long, black hair around the barrel of the curling iron. "Then you can put on your dress."

"I could have just used a glamour spell for her hair," I said.

Serena scoffed. "This is the best part of getting ready for a dance. It's cheating if you use a spell."

"I don't mind how long it's taking," Zoie said. "It's kind of fun. I haven't curled my hair like this since the last dance."

"Your dress and shoes are on the bed," I said.

"Jewelry?" Serena asked.

"All together and on my nightstand," Zoie said.

"Flip your head," Serena commanded. "Let's get you some volume, and then finger comb those curls."

As Serena put the finishing touches on Zoie's hair, I sat down on the edge of Zoie's bed and looked around the room. A room that used to be mine when I was growing up. My dad called it the Princess Tower. When he had the castle built for my mom, he said every princess needed her own tower. I'd spent every day of my life up until I left the island sleeping in the tower—and now Zoie was doing the same.

I couldn't be happier.

"Well?" Serena asked, turning Zoie around to face me. "What do you think?"

"Beautiful." I stood and strolled over to them. "Let me see the back."

Zoie turned her head, giving me a view of the back where her soft curls were held together with a faux-diamond barrette shaped like a witch's hat.

I chuckled. "Nice touch."

"Dad gave it to me." Zoie turned back around. "Does my makeup look okay?"

"Perfect." I motioned to her dress. "Let's get you ready. Brick will be here in about fifteen minutes."

"Luckily, The Spellmoore isn't too far from here," Serena said as I helped Zoie slip the red slinky dress over her head. "Shouldn't take you guys too long to get there."

"I haven't been to The Spellmoore since your wedding, Serena." Zoie lifted her hair so I could zip the back of her dress. "I can't wait to see how they decorated the banquet room."

Headlights flashed across Zoie's walls, and I met Serena's excited eyes over Zoie's head.

"I bet that's Brick. Serena and I will be downstairs waiting for you." I pointed to the jewelry she had on her nightstand. "Can you get the rest of this on your own?"

Zoie nodded. "I can. See you downstairs."

Serena and I linked arms and strode down the hallway and descended the wide, curved staircase. Needles hovered near the door, his wings glowing red and gold.

"Get away from there!" I scolded as we reached the bottom of the staircase. "Even Alex isn't being that irrational."

"I wouldn't exactly say that," Alex said, moving up behind me and slipping his arms around my waist. "I'm just holding it in better."

The doorbell rang, and I all but sprinted for the door. The last thing Brick needed was to come face-to-face with Needles.

Motioning him back with a flick of my wrist, I opened the door.

"Brick, come on in," I gushed. "Don't you look dashing in your tux."

Serena clapped her hands together. "And I love how your cummerbund and tie match Zoie's red rhinestone dress."

Brick self-consciously smoothed down the front of his shirt. "That was all Zoie's and Izzy's idea. They wanted us all to match."

"You look nice, son." Alex stuck out his hand to Brick. "You excited?"

Brick transferred the box holding Zoie's wrist corsage to his other hand before clasping Alex's. "I am. It's all Zoie's been talking about for the last two weeks."

Needles landed on my shoulder, and I groaned. He'd pulled a quill from his back and was using a miniature sword to sharpen the quill. Not that the quill needed it, but it was still intimidating.

Brick glanced at Needles, then nervously cleared his throat. "Is Zoie about ready?"

"Stop it," I hissed.

Serena laughed. "Don't worry, Brick. Needles is just being Needles."

"Are you being mean to my boyfriend?" Zoie asked from the top of the stairs.

We all looked up and did a collective gasp. Zoie looked absolutely stunning in the floor-length red sequined dress. The front dipped low enough that when Alex first saw it, he'd nearly had a heart attack. But he came around when he saw how excited Zoie was, and how the dress truly seemed to be made to fit her *and* her sparkling personality.

"I'll get the boutonniere," I said. "Serena, can you get the camera?"

I hurried to the kitchen to grab Brick's boutonniere out of the refrigerator. Seeing Alex's glass of wine on the counter, I took a healthy gulp. I hadn't been this nervous in ages.

"Now remember," Zoie said as I walked back into the foyer. "I'm spending the night in town with Izzy. We'll all be home by one. No need to worry."

"I'm the dad," Alex said. "It's my job to worry."

"And it's my job to protect," Needles said, still sharpening his quill.

I handed Zoie the boutonniere, hoping to distract her enough she wouldn't argue with Needles. Once Brick's flower was pinned, and Zoie's wrist corsage was on, we spent a few minutes taking pictures and having fun.

"You two run along," Alex said. "Have fun, but be safe."

Zoie leaned over and kissed her dad on the cheek. "We will. Shayla, don't let Dad worry too much."

I looped an arm around Alex's. "I'll try."

When the front door closed behind the two, Serena patted her stomach. "Well, I think it's time baby and I went home. I took a short nap before I got here, but I'm tired again."

I gave her a quick hug. "You drove, right?"

Serena snorted. "Yes, can you believe that? I'm not even a mile away, and I can't seem to drag myself up here."

"Give yourself a break. Go home, snuggle up to that handsome werewolf of yours, and relax the rest of the night."

"What will you guys do?" she asked.

I slipped my hand into Alex's and squeezed. "I want to go see Dad real quick."

* * *

Alex and I held hands as we traversed the dirt path behind my house that led to Black Forest. Technically, I guess the path now led to Mom's cottage *and* Black Forest. We were almost at Mom's place when the fireflies swooped down on us.

"Princess, are you and Alex coming to see Black Forest King?"

"How is Serena's baby?"

"I'm so excited about the wedding."

"Your mom is sitting on her front porch in the rocking chair Black Forest King had made for her."

The fireflies continued to chatter until Needles sent them scampering away with a harsh rebuke. *"It's impossible to think straight with those magpies around."*

Alex squeezed my hand, and I almost laughed outright. I wasn't about to tell Needles that was exactly how it was sometimes with him around.

When we passed by mom's house, she waved to us from her front porch. "Going to see your father?"

"Yep. You wanna come? Or have you already seen him today?"

"You two go on ahead. I saw your dad earlier." Mom smiled. "I'm still getting used to saying that."

Waving goodbye, we continued down the path to Black Forest. Since the fireflies were gone, I conjured up a light orb and tossed it in the air. I missed the glowing light I usually had on my walk.

It didn't take long before we stood in front of my favorite pine tree. He was so big, his thick branches nearly brushed the forest floor. And because he knew what an honor it was to be in that position, he stood tall and resolute at the entrance to Black Forest.

"Hello, Mr. Pine," I said, extinguishing the orb. "May we enter and visit with Dad?"

"You know you never have to ask permission, Princess. Black Forest will always be your home." The pine tree lifted his heavy branches off the ground, granting us entrance. *"Enjoy your time in Black Forest. I do so love seeing Serenity visit. Reminds me of when she was a young woman walking these woods and Black Forest King first saw her."*

"I'm glad too," I said.

Entering Black Forest was akin to nirvana. Not only was it beautiful, but it was peaceful and calm as well. It was like no other place in the world I'd ever been to. I'd always thought it was because I was *literally* a part of Black Forest, but Alex once assured me he also felt the same way when he entered.

The three of us took off immediately—Alex and I jogging, weaving between the trees, and laughing at the antics of the fireflies and other forest animals. When we came to a small clearing, we finally slowed down until we stood in front of the most magnificent tree in all of Black Forest.

My dad.

His tree roots were at least four feet tall off the ground and extended out about twenty feet from the base of his trunk. He was nearly one hundred twenty feet around, with branches averaging thirty to forty feet. He was the largest tree in Black Forest...and nothing could shake him.

Dad was a Genius Loci, which meant he was literally the heart and soul of the forest.

"Hello, Shayla." Dad's deep voice reverberated inside my head. *"I am pleased you and Alex Stone have come for a visit. Your mother was also here today to visit."*

"We saw her sitting in the rocking chair you made her." I jumped up onto one of his roots and ran down the length of him until I was at his trunk. Wrapping my arms around him as much as I could, I gave him a hug. "I've missed you."

"And I have missed you, Daughter of my Heart. Sit and tell me what is new on the island."

Alex came to a stop behind me, and we both dropped to the ground to sit at the base of Dad's trunk. Needles zipped up into Dad's branches, getting lost in his massiveness.

"I'm afraid it's not good," Alex said.

"Yes, Serenity has told me a little of what is going on." Dad sighed. *"Another murder?"*

"I'm afraid so." I leaned back and rested against him and filled him in on everything we knew so far about the case.

"I am sure you two and Needles will be able to solve your mystery. Now, let us talk about something more pleasant. Young Zoie is at her dance tonight, yes?"

"Yep." I slipped my hand into Alex's. "Brick picked her up not long ago. In fact, they're probably at the dance by now."

"And how are you holding up, Alex Stone? I may not have been able to see Shayla off on these momentous nights, but it does not mean I did not worry."

I knew Dad regretted not being able to be a part of my life when it came to things like dances, dates, graduations, and other important events. That was why I made sure our wedding would take place in Black Forest. I didn't want Dad to ever feel like he was being left out again.

"I like Brick," Alex said. "He's proven to be a trustworthy young man. I'm sure the two will have a good time tonight."

"It will be hard on Young Zoie when Brick moves away to attend college. Hopefully, the anticipation of a new baby and the wedding in a few months will help ease her pain."

"That's my hope as well," I said.

"I hate to cut this short," Alex said, "but Shayla and I still need to do one last thing tonight. Just a quick stakeout."

"He's going to fly us to the northwest side of the island."

"And me!" Needles slowly drifted down from Dad's branches. *"You aren't leaving me behind."*

Alex groaned. "We won't be long, Needles. There's no need for—"

"Where Shayla goes…I go." Needles' wings glowed purple. *"That's how it is, Gargoyle."*

"He's not going on the honeymoon," Alex said. "I know I've said it before, but I mean it. I draw the line there."

"We'll see, Gargoyle. We'll see," Needles taunted.

Dad chuckled. *"Have fun, you three. And be safe."*

❧ 14 ❧

The minute Alex set me on my feet and retracted his wings, Needles shot out from under my collar.

"Let's have a drink and grill some suspects."

I thanked Alex as he opened the front door to Bites & Beer. It was only seven o'clock on a Saturday night, but inside it was already lively and loud.

"If we're lucky," Alex said as Needles shot ahead of us, "not only will Henry Vampton be here, but so will Beau and Ellen. I'm curious to see how those two interact."

"Whaddya thinking?" I asked. "Affair?"

Alex shook his head and guided me into the dimly lit bar. "I don't know. It seems like an unlikely pairing, but…"

His voice trailed off, and when he didn't continue, I finished his thought. "You're thinking given how eager Ellen is to have a baby, maybe she figures he's her best bet?"

Alex scoffed. "Doesn't say much for the male population on the island."

I grinned and winked at him. "Serena, Tamara, and I definitely got the pick of the litter."

Needles rocketed back to where we stood, his wings glowing orange with excitement. *"We are in luck. Not only is Beau working behind the bar, but Ellen is sitting at the counter having drinks. I sneaked over to Henry's office and peered through his keyhole. He's sitting behind his desk working."*

"Let's talk with Henry first," Alex said.

We followed Needles across the room to a door marked OFFICE, and Alex knocked soundly.

"I'll go spy on Beau and Ellen while you two pick this vampire's brain."

Needles flew away as the door was yanked open by a tall, beefy troll.

"No patrons allowed," his voice boomed, deep and surly.

"I'm Sheriff Stone, and this is my associate Shayla Loci. We need to speak to Henry Vampton."

The troll stared down at us, unblinking and unsmiling. "No patrons allowed."

"It's okay, Brutus. Let them in."

Henry Vampton leaned back in his chair and steepled his fingers, assessing us as we entered. He was dressed in a midnight blue suit with no tie, and his black hair was slicked back off his face, enhancing his dark eyes and square chin.

"Please, come in and sit down." He rose and motioned to the two chairs in front of his desk before sitting back down. "Brutus, why don't you go out to the bar floor and make sure everyone is behaving themselves."

Brutus nodded once, then strode out the door, shutting it soundly behind him.

"He doesn't say much, but he keeps the peace." Henry smiled, flashing us his fangs. "My wife informed me you two dropped by our house earlier today to talk about Charlotte Stoneman's death. I'm afraid I had to be here to sign for a shipment, so I missed you. What can I help you with?"

"Friday night between nine and midnight," Alex said. "Were you here at the bar?"

Henry nodded. "I was. I came in around seven, about the time Ellen left to attend Charlotte's party, and I didn't leave until after one."

I furrowed my brow. "You knew your wife was attending Charlotte's going away party?"

"I did."

"You didn't think that was odd?" I mused. "Ellen, herself, told us you were angry because she'd spent so much money at Charlotte's store, and that Charlotte even called you to tell you she would not be selling any more jewelry or charms to Ellen."

Henry shrugged. "What was I supposed to do? Stop my wife from going? I assumed she had an invitation to the party."

"Ellen told us after she left the party she came here to Bites & Beer," Alex said. "Do you know what time your wife arrived?"

Henry narrowed his eyes. "You want to know if she had time to kill Charlotte, is that correct? Trust me, my wife might be a little—well, let's just say she can be a little obsessive when it comes to having a baby, but she's not going to kill Charlotte over it."

Thinking about how Ellen wanted to yank out one of Needles' wings, I wasn't so sure I agreed with him.

"That didn't answer my question," Alex said. "Do you know what time your wife arrived at the bar last night?"

Henry leaned forward, resting his elbows on the desk. "I don't know for sure. I came out of my office a little before ten since that's when the crowd picks up, and she was already sitting at the bar having a drink. I have no idea how long she'd been there."

"What about Beau Broombotten?" Alex mused. "Was he here last night?"

Henry glanced up at the ceiling. "Beau? Yes, but he showed up after I saw my wife. I'd say maybe ten minutes had passed before he came strolling in."

"So he may have arrived around ten or ten-fifteen?" I asked.

Henry nodded. "I'd say that sounds about right. We were pretty busy, so he stepped behind the counter for a little while to help out." He shuffled around on his desk and pulled out a piece of paper. "Yes. I have him down working from ten to one."

"And what time do you close?" Alex asked.

"Two on Friday and Saturday. The rest of the week, we close by eleven."

Alex stood, and I followed suit.

"Thank you for your time, Mr. Vampton. I think Shayla and I will have a drink before we head back home, if that's okay?"

Henry Vampton stood and smiled. "Of course. Enjoy yourselves. Most nights it's pretty quiet, except for the weekends. But it won't get too rowdy in here until around ten."

Alex and I exited the office and made a beeline toward the bar. Beau and Ellen had their heads together and were in a deep conversation when we approached. It wasn't until Beau lifted his head that he even notice us, and when he did, his eyes went wide. He jumped back so quickly, he almost tripped over his own feet. Ellen swiveled in her chair to see what had him so panicked.

"Hello," I said, sitting down on the vacant barstool next to her. "Alex and I thought we might drop in and have a drink."

Ellen's eyes darted to her husband's office. "I thought I answered all your questions this morning."

"We didn't come here to talk to you. We came here to talk to your husband." I smiled at Beau. "I'll take a jalapeno margarita."

A look passed between Beau and Ellen, but I couldn't decipher its meaning.

"One jalapeno margarita coming up." Beau glanced at Alex standing behind my barstool. "And you?"

"Nothing for me."

"I'll have a Scotch straight up," Needles said as he perched on my shoulder.

I reached out and grabbed a handful of pretzels and passed them to Needles. "No, you won't. You can have a pretzel and that's it."

"You're about as much fun as a deflated balloon, Princess."

I glanced down the counter and saw someone I recognized. A few months back, Alex and I had to come into Bites & Beer to get the alibi of another suspect we'd had. The bartender had answered all our questions and even made friends with Needles. Catching his eye, I lifted my hand and waved.

"Hey," the bartender called out. "Nice to see you guys back. Be sure and hook them up, Beau."

Beau grunted. "Yeah, right."

"I can't believe you brought that *animal* inside the bar," Ellen sniffed. "Beau, isn't there an ordinance against such things? Should it be here in the bar?"

Beau snorted. "Seriously, Ellen? It's an island full of supernaturals. Technically, shifters are animals." He turned and proceeded to fix my drink while Needles chomped away in my ear.

Ellen sighed and took a sip from her glass. "Why are you really here?"

"Like I said, we just wanted to ask your husband a couple questions." I smiled at Beau when he set my drink in front of me.

I took a small sip and smiled. “Delicious.” I rotated my fingertip clockwise above the drink, using my magic to swirl the icy beverage. “You two seemed to be enthralled in your conversation. I hope we didn’t interrupt anything important?”

“Not at all,” Ellen snapped as she slammed her drink down on the counter and slid off her barstool. “If you’ll excuse me, I need to go speak to my husband.”

I watched in amusement as she lifted her nose in the air and stalked away from us.

“Was it something I said?” I joked.

Beau scowled. “I got others to wait on.”

“Don’t let us stop you,” I said, taking another sip of my drink.

Beau looked from me to Alex, then turned on his heel and walked away.

“I’d say those two were acting a might suspicious,” Alex mused.

“Couldn’t agree more. And the fact both of them were here at the bar between nine-fifty and ten still puts them in the timeline to have killed Charlotte.” I took another drink of my margarita and pushed back from the counter. “I’m exhausted and ready to call it a night.”

Alex tossed some cash onto the bar. “Then let’s go home.”

15

"I *hate working Sundays*," Needles grumbled from the backseat of Alex's Blazer. "*The bakery isn't open, so no caramel pretzel to start my day.*"

I rummaged around in my bag and handed him a pretzel from the plastic baggie I kept for emergencies. "Suck it up. You're supposed to be a warrior, remember?"

Alex snickered, but wisely kept his mouth shut.

"Besides," I continued, "it's ten-thirty. You already had breakfast, and we're having lunch with GiGi in about an hour and a half."

"*If I last that long.*"

Euthelva and Annaleigh lived on the east side of town on Ghost Galley Way. The street-lined homes in this section had a historical feel to them—two stories, lots of pitched roofs, wide front porches, and even larger front and back yards. I could see why Annaleigh and Charlotte chose to stay in the location and just build a small cottage of their own behind Euthelva's house for more independence.

There were two cars in the driveway. I recognized the one as Euthelva's car, so I guessed the other to be Annaleigh's. Alex parked behind Annaleigh's vehicle, and we exited the Blazer.

Euthelva's porch was lined with hanging philodendrons and ivy. Needles buzzed from plant to plant, inspecting the leaves and soil. I didn't bother to tell him he was wasting his time. The moment I stepped up onto the porch, I could feel the joy radiating from them. Well, from all but one.

I reached out and touched the blackened end of one of the philodendron's leaves. Whispering a healing spell, I smiled as the black leaf turned green.

"Thank you," the plant whispered.

Alex knocked on the door as Needles perched on my shoulder. A few seconds later, Euthelva answered the door, looking polished and sophisticated in cream linen pants and an emerald green shirt. She motioned us inside with the coffee cup in her hand.

"Good morning, Sheriff." Her eyes traveled to me and then Needles perched on my shoulder. "Shayla. And this must be your partner I've heard rumors of."

Needles' wings fluttered in my ear, and I smiled at Euthelva. "Yes. This is Needles."

"Well, come on in. Annaleigh is in the kitchen. We're goi—" She broke off and cleared her throat. "We're going over funeral arrangements. We did a little last night, but it was just too overwhelming."

"We won't take up too much of your time," Alex said. "We understand you're busy."

Annaleigh sat at the kitchen table, staring blankly into her coffee cup, a small notepad and pen in front of her. She looked up when I took the chair opposite her. Alex stood next to Euthelva by the coffee maker.

"How're you doing, Annaleigh?" I asked.

Annaleigh snorted. "How do you think I'm doing? I'm supposed to be helping my cousin pack and later take her to the airport. Instead, I'm planning for her funeral." A tear slipped down her cheek, and she brushed it aside before taking a drink from her mug.

"I'm very sorry."

"Is it true?" she demanded. "Did Charlotte die from a death spell?"

"Yes."

"How can that be?" Euthelva demanded from the counter. "Death spells aren't performed anymore. I don't know of a single witch who'd knowingly weave a death spell."

"That's what we're trying to find out," I said.

Alex slid a mug of coffee in front of me, and then he and Euthelva sat down in the empty chairs around the table. For something to do, and to give Annaleigh time to compose herself, I picked up the cream and sugar and doctored my coffee.

"If this isn't hard enough to deal with," Annaleigh continued, "Charlotte's boyfriend, James, is flying in today." She picked up her mug and swirled her coffee. "I'm to pick him up at two from the airstrip."

"Alex and I would love to talk with him," I said.

"Why?" Annaleigh asked. "He doesn't know anything about the murder."

"Maybe, maybe not," Alex said. "It could be Charlotte said something to him about someone stalking her or wanting to harm her."

Annaleigh shrugged. "I suppose. James and I sort of talked about that a little yesterday on the phone. He has no clue who did this, but I'm sure he wouldn't mind talking to you. I'm taking him straight from the airport to the morgue." Her voice broke, and she cleared her throat. "Maybe we can talk with you then?"

"Count me out." Needles' wings glowed blue and gray. *"No way am I hanging out in a room with dead bodies."*

The morgue was really just a side room in Doc's laboratory where family members could view the body in private.

"That would be great," Alex said. "We'll meet you around two at the station."

"What will happen to Charming Baubles now?" I asked. "The building, I mean."

Annaleigh shrugged. "I honestly don't know. At one point, Charlotte had it in her will that the shop and building would go to me when she died. I assume there's a clause or something in the will that says if she sells the building beforehand, then it's void or something, but I really don't know. We're meeting with Charlotte's lawyer tomorrow to go over all that." She looked up at me and gave me a wry smile. "I *can* tell you Grey is wondering the same thing. He called about half an hour ago, wanting to get together tonight to talk. I told him I wouldn't know anything until tomorrow after we spoke to the lawyer, but he was insistent. So I agreed."

Euthelva sighed. "He'll probably try to hold Annaleigh to the agreement he made with Charlotte."

"Maybe that wouldn't be such a bad thing." Annaleigh let out a small bark of laughter. "I mean, what am I going to do with a magical jewelry shop? I can't do elemental magic, and neither can you."

"That's not the point," Euthelva said. "Charlotte left that shop to you originally, so you should keep it going. She would have wanted it that way."

Annaleigh shrugged and looked out the window. "I guess."

"Who's her lawyer?" I asked.

"Xavier Oakman," Annaleigh said. "He's with Greenly, Witchington, & Oakman."

I nodded. "I know Xavier. He was a few grades under me in school."

I didn't add Xavier had helped us out in a couple of our other cases already, so I knew he'd tell us what we needed to know.

"I need to ask you something, Annaleigh," Alex said. "We did a background check on you, and it came back you were once arrested for assault."

Annaleigh gasped. "You ran a background check on me? Why?"

Euthelva sighed. "Because they think maybe we had something to do with Charlotte's death."

Annaleigh jumped up from the table. "That's insane! I'd *never* hurt Charlotte. I loved her! We answered all your questions Friday night and pointed you to other suspects."

"Convenient," Needles murmured in my ear.

"Sit down, Annaleigh," Euthelva said soothingly. "They wouldn't be doing their job if they didn't check us out."

"But—but, I didn't hurt her. I couldn't kill Charlotte. I mean, like I *really* couldn't kill her." She sat down at the table. "I can't do magic. And everyone knows a death spell requires magic."

I didn't point out she could easily use the dark supernatural Internet to get a potion already made up. "We just need to know about the assault charges."

Annaleigh rolled her eyes and took a drink of her coffee. "It was awful. It was the first big convention Charlotte and I ever attended." She gave a small smile. "We only had like thirty pieces of jewelry made at the time, but we thought we were so big flying to the mainland to sell our jewelry at a big supernatural gathering." She took a drink of her coffee. "It happened our last night there. Believe it or not, there are still supernaturals out there prejudiced against Normals. I know it even happens here on Enchanted Island, but I didn't really encounter much of it growing up. But at the convention—well, let's just say when word got out I was a Normal, not everyone was accepting. I had a bunch of people tell me I should leave, and when one got pushy, I pushed back." She smiled. "Like literally pushed back. I don't know why I got physical with this guy. I really don't. I just remember being so angry, and even though Charlotte kept assuring me their opinions meant nothing, I just couldn't take it any longer. It was three days of constant antagonism. When that guy got in my face, I grabbed the closest thing to me—which happened to be a leaded crystal ball from another vendor's table—and I just whacked him over the head."

"I still don't understand what got into you," Euthelva said. "You aren't that person."

"I never thought I was, either. Until I was pushed to the point I couldn't take it anymore." Annaleigh sighed and took another sip of her coffee. "Needless to say, the supernatural police on duty at the convention came and arrested me. Charlotte tried to explain what had happened and why I struck the guy, but when they heard I was a Normal and that I'd struck a supernatural out of anger…" Her voice trailed off. "Well, let's just say I was immediately shown the inside of the local supernatural jail cell."

"But you were able to get the charges lowered?" I mused.

"Yeah. Luckily, the prosecuting attorney had a son who was Normal, and so he understood when I explained what happened. He said he couldn't make the charges go away completely, but he could see what he could do about getting them lowered."

"Thanks for telling us," I said softly. "I'm sure it was difficult."

Annaleigh scoffed. "You have *no* idea how difficult it is to live among the supernatural and not be able to do what they do. And then to have them look down on you…it's just awful."

I reached over and laid my hand over hers. "Not everyone feels that way, Annaleigh."

She blinked back tears and withdrew her hand. "I know. I get that. And I have a lot of friends who are supernaturals. But it doesn't mean it doesn't hurt."

I wasn't sure how to respond.

"Can I get you a refill on your coffees?" Euthelva asked, breaking the awkward silence.

Alex stood from the table. "No, thanks. Shayla and I don't want to keep you any longer."

Standing, I leaned over and gave Annaleigh a hug. "I'll see you at the sheriff's station around two."

Annaleigh nodded. "Sure."

"Let me show you out," Euthelva said.

When we reached the front door, Euthelva put her hand on my arm. "Thank you for that. Annaleigh has always been sensitive about being a Normal, and it was usually Charlotte who either stood up for her or calmed her down."

"Well, I meant it. It doesn't matter to me if she's a Normal or not. She's still a person who deserves respect."

"That was kind of you, Princess," Needles said when the door closed behind us.

"I spoke the truth," I said.

Once back in the Blazer, Alex called Xavier's private cell number and put him on speakerphone.

"I figured I'd get a call from you eventually," Xavier said. "How can I help you? I assume this is about Charlotte Stoneman's death?"

"Sorry to bother you on a Sunday," Alex said. "We just need to know if Charlotte changed her will within the last few weeks, or if Annaleigh will inherit the business and building like she believes."

"Charlotte did not change her will. As of right now, Annaleigh will inherit the business and everything it entails, along with the building."

Needles perched on my headrest. *"Not looking good for Annaleigh."*

"Thanks, Xavier." Alex disconnected and shoved his phone in his shirt pocket.

"Doesn't prove anything," I said.

But my protest sounded lame even to me.

16

Alex did a quick safety sweep of the town before driving to GiGi's—which used to be Mom's house—for lunch. Even though I hated the fact GiGi no longer lived down the lane from me, I was glad we still had a family member in town. It made food stops easier.

"Hey, GiGi," I called out as we strolled through the front room into the kitchen. "Smells good. Hope you got enough for one more. Zoie's coming over."

I'd called Zoie during our patrol of the town and invited her to GiGi's for lunch. She'd sounded perkier than I expected, seeing as how I was pretty sure she and Izzy had gotten virtually zero sleep after they got home from prom. Eager to tell us about her night, she said she'd head right over.

GiGi looked up from the counter and scowled. "I forgot to pick up the Saskatoon berries. Can you believe that?"

"What's a Saskatoon berry?" I asked. "Alex and I can run and pick it up for you."

GiGi snorted. "How're you gonna do that when you don't know what it is?"

I rolled my eyes. "I'm sure someone at the store can help me."

GiGi threw up her hands. "Bah! I trust those workers about as much as I trust Needles alone with a bag of pretzels."

"Smart woman." Needles landed on the mixer. *"No bag of pretzels is safe around me."*

I laughed. "Fair enough. I'll ride to the grocery store with you so you can introduce me to this Saskatoon berry."

"Needles and I will stay here and wait for Zoie," Alex said.

"And Byron," GiGi added. "He's coming for lunch as well."

"Byron is?" I waggled my eyebrows. "Getting awfully serious with him, aren't you?"

"Hush up," GiGi snapped. "Or I'll hex you good, granddaughter or not."

"I like him," Alex said. "He seems very level-headed."

Which was code for Byron would keep GiGi grounded when she flew off the deep end.

GiGi snatched up her keys off a pegboard, and I groaned.

"Not the Princess Lolly!" I pleaded.

The Princess Lolly was a two-person vehicle made to look like something the Candyland princess would drive. It was cotton candy pink with yellow and orange lollipops welded onto the roof. While incredibly tiny, it *was* street legal and topped out at fifty miles per hour. Recently, it had been involved in a wreck, but shifter weasel Weston down at Weston's Auto Body was able to fix her up and make her look like new.

GiGi cackled and did a little jig. "I never thought I'd say it, but I'm really liking this car. Gets me lots of attention, and I love that."

Fifteen minutes later, Gigi and I were standing in the produce section looking over the Saskatoon berries on display. They looked exactly like a blueberry, I thought.

"So, you're basically making a blueberry pie?" I asked.

GiGi scoffed. "There's a huge difference between a blueberry and a Saskatoon berry. Besides, this pie I'm making has rhubarb *and* Saskatoon berries in it. It is *not* a blueberry pie."

I held up my hands and backed away. "Sorry. Didn't mean to offend you or the Saskatoon berry."

GiGi snorted, and after a thorough inspection, dropped each berry into the bag. When it looked like she was finished, I turned and started for the checkout counter.

"Wait," GiGi said. "I got one more thing to do."

"What?"

"It won't take long."

We strolled through the produce area, waving and greeting other shoppers. It wasn't until GiGi headed toward the fish and meat counter that I realized her true intention.

"No. Come on, GiGi. We don't have time for this."

GiGi grinned. "There's always time to mess with a bully."

It was on the tip of my tongue to tell her that her intended target wasn't being the bully...*she* was. But that would probably just get me zapped with some magic. So I wisely kept my mouth shut as GiGi strolled slowly by the fish display.

"What're you doing here, Witch?" the large werewolf shifter behind the display case snarled.

"Just looking at your Chilean sea bass," GiGi said innocently. "Thought I might pick me up a piece." She grinned widely, showing her teeth. "Or maybe a slab of salmon."

Werewolf shifter, Morris Wulfton, growled low in his chest. "You know I don't serve you fish. You're not welcome here."

GiGi slapped a hand against her chest in mock despair,

glancing at the customers around her. "What? You're refusing to serve an old woman like me? A harmless old witch?"

I couldn't hold back the laughter that bubbled up inside me. Calling GiGi a harmless old witch was a huge stretch, and even GiGi had to know she was laying it on pretty thick.

Over a year ago, GiGi and Morris had locked horns over Morris' belief that Normals were not true supernaturals, but abominations. GiGi had responded by using her magic to yank a long salmon filet out of the display case and slapping it over Morris' mouth and half his head. The man had fainted on the spot. Not something a werewolf could easily live down.

"Harmless my you-know-what!" Morris snarled. "Now, go on and get outta here."

"Don't be such a beast," a customer called out. "Give GiGi her fish."

Grinning like an idiot, GiGi pointed to a thick piece of Chilean sea bass. "I'll take that one right there."

Once Gigi had her fun at Morris' expense, we paid for the berries and fish and headed back to her place. She'd just passed Charming Baubles when I frowned and whipped my head around and stared back at the building.

"GiGi, stop the car."

"What's going on?" she demanded. "Robbery in progress? We got some dirtbags to take down?"

I rolled my eyes. "No. I thought I saw something in the alley behind Charlotte's building. Let's go take a look."

GiGi parked the Princess Lolly along the curb in front of Betty's Boo-tique. Crossing the street, we hurried down the side alley to the back of Charlotte's building. I wasn't sure who was more surprised—me, or the two people standing by the back door.

"What's going on?" I demanded.

Beau Broombotten shrugged. "Not much. Ellen was driving by and thought she saw someone inside the store. So she called me, and I offered to come take a look."

GiGi snorted. "That's so dumb, it's insulting. You couldn't think of something better than that?"

Ellen Vampton's face turned red. "It's the truth. I didn't have Annaleigh's number, so I called Beau."

I crossed my arms over my chest. "And not the sheriff's department?"

Ellen's eyes slid away from me, and she shrugged. "I wasn't thinking straight."

"And me being the gentleman I am, I ran right over to make sure nothing was wrong with Charlotte's place."

GiGi sniffed. "You don't think I can't smell magic, boy? Nothing good is going on here."

"Come on, Beau." Ellen tugged at Beau's sleeve. "Obviously, they don't care we're concerned citizens."

I let out a bark of laughter. "Concerned citizens? Really?"

Ellen continued to tug Beau down the alley...his eyes never leaving mine until they turned the corner.

GiGi put her hand on the back door. "I think he was using magic to try and break through the ward on the shop."

I nodded. "Probably right. We just don't have any proof to arrest them."

"Then let's get home. The Saskatoon berries won't keep forever."

As GiGi drove back to her place, I thought about why Beau and Ellen were trying to break into Charlotte's store. All my answers circled back to them somehow being involved with Charlotte's murder.

17

By the time Zoie ran out of steam, and we finished our meal, it was almost two o'clock. Zoie offered to stay and help GiGi and Byron with the dishes before flying back to the castle.

"I just hope no one sees me," she joked. "Do you know how weird I'll look flying home carrying a prom dress?"

"I think I'll go back with Zoie," Needles said, yawning hugely. *"You're just going to the dead room and then back home, right?"*

I nodded. "Yes. The morgue and then home."

"You don't mind flying me to the castle, do you, Miss Zoie?"

"Not at all."

Alex and I thanked GiGi—making sure to praise her Saskatoon berry pie—and headed to the sheriff's station. Parking in front of the building behind Annaleigh's vehicle, we entered and went downstairs to Doc's lab. I was a little disappointed the surly Pearl wasn't behind her desk giving us a hard time, but it was Sunday, and she was probably home snuggled up with her husband.

Alex knocked once on the door before pushing it open.

Doc peaked his head out from the side room and met us halfway. “I have Annaleigh and the boyfriend, James, viewing the body now.”

“Have they been here long?” Alex asked.

Doc shook his head. “I’d say maybe ten minutes.”

We made small talk as we waited for Annaleigh and James to finish. A few minutes later, the two walked back into Doc’s laboratory.

“Oh,” Annaleigh said. “I didn’t know you guys were here. James, this is our sheriff, Alex Stone. And this is Shayla Loci, our game warden. They’re looking into Charlotte’s death.”

“Sorry to meet you under these circumstances.” Alex stuck out his hand and the two men shook. “We’d like to ask you a few questions.”

James ran his hands through his sandy-colored hair, causing the ends to stick up. Despite the sorrow etched on his face, he was a handsome man with cobalt blue eyes, dark lashes, and a square jaw. “Of course. I’ll be honest, Sheriff. I have no idea who could have killed Charlotte.” He closed his eyes briefly. “I’ve been told it was a death spell.”

“Yes,” Alex said.

“Charlotte never said anything to me about being afraid of anyone,” James continued. “Well, except her ex-boyfriend, but as far as I knew, he hadn’t really been around lately.”

Annaleigh frowned. “That’s not exactly true. I just think she didn’t want to worry you.”

“When was the last time you spoke to Charlotte?” Alex asked.

“Friday night. Right before she left to go to the party.”

I furrowed my brow. “You guys didn’t text or anything throughout the night?”

James shook his head, tears in his eyes. "No. I wanted Charlotte to have that time with her friends."

"How long had you two been dating?" Alex asked.

"Seriously dating for about six months. Of course, it was long distance, which was why Charlotte was moving. We were ready to take the next step."

"Are you staying on the island?" I asked.

Annaleigh rested her hand on James' arm. "I'm staying with mom so James can stay in the cottage."

Alex nodded. "Good. If I have any more questions, I know how to reach you." Alex turned to Doc. "Thank you for coming in and making time for us."

"Yes," James said. "I appreciate you letting me see Charlotte one last time."

Annaleigh looked away and swiped at her eyes.

Doc smiled sadly at James. "I'm sorry for your loss."

"Shayla and I will walk you out," Alex said. "I take it that's your car in front of the station?"

Annaleigh nodded. "Yes."

We said goodbye to Doc, and the four of us traipsed upstairs and back outside. Alex had just shut and locked the front door when a vehicle slid to a stop in front of us, tires squealing. Directly behind him was Deputy Sparks in his patrol car, lights flashing.

"How dare you show your face on this island!" Beau shouted, leaping from his vehicle. "It's because of you Charlotte's dead. If she wouldn't have had that stupid going away party, she'd still be alive."

Beau lunged for James' throat, but Alex stepped in front of him. Deputy Sparks jumped out of his vehicle, hand on his weapon.

"Step back, Beau," Alex demanded, holding out his hand.

But Beau wasn't listening. He drew back a fist and let it fly. Alex must have expected the move because he shifted into his gargoyle form and didn't even flinch when Beau's fist hit his stone jaw. Beau doubled over, screaming in pain. I was pretty sure he'd just broken his hand.

"I think my hand is broken!" Beau yelled. "You broke my hand!"

Alex shifted back to his human form and grunted. "I didn't do anything. You, on the other hand, just hit a law enforcement officer." He turned to Deputy Sparks. "Take him inside. Let him cool down in a cell for a while."

Deputy Sparks nodded, then grabbed Beau by the back of his shirt and shoved the screaming man toward the front door.

Annaleigh clucked her tongue and shook her head. "Well, Sheriff, that should be all the proof you need that Beau Broombotten is someone who could get angry enough to crush someone's windpipe."

18

"I want to see what Beau's next move is," Alex said.

Zoie was using her magic to clear off the dinner table and put the dishes in the sink. For some reason, it always reminded me of the cartoon version of *Beauty & the Beast*... when all the dishes were singing and dancing and flying around the table as Belle ate her dinner.

"What do you suggest?" I asked, wincing when one of the dishes faltered and landed with a crash in the sink.

"Oops," Zoie said. "I'll clean it up."

"I think Beau's cooled down enough," Alex said. "I'll text Deputy Sparks and let him know we're coming in to release him. Then you and I will follow him and see where he goes."

"Where do you think he'll go?" I asked.

"After what you told me about seeing him and Ellen behind Charming Baubles, it wouldn't surprise me if he tries to break in again." He grinned. "I want to be there when he does."

"Me too!" Needles zipped over to where we stood near the sink, his wings humming loudly. *"I'm up for a stakeout."*

"Guess I'll bring the pretzels," I joked.

"We'll take your Bronco, so it's not obvious." Alex turned to his daughter. "You don't mind if we go out for a while, do you?"

"Gosh, no. I'm exhausted. I'm going upstairs, taking a bath, and then going straight to bed. I got school in the morning."

"I'm just not sure of the connection between trying to get into the store and killing Charlotte," I said.

"Me neither," Alex admitted, "but it's something to go on."

By the time we reached the sheriff's station, it was nearing eight o'clock. The sun had just set, and the street was empty and dark except for the sporadic streetlight. Beau's vehicle was still parked along the street at a precarious angle. Alex opened the door for Needles and me, and we made our way down the hall to the sheriff's office.

"Evening, Sheriff. Shayla. Needles." Deputy Sparks dropped his feet off his desk and slowly stood. "Slow night tonight. Nice and quiet in town and around the island, it seems."

"Hey!" Beau yelled out from the jail cell not ten feet away. "You gonna let me out of here or what? I got rights, ya know!" He shook his hand in the air. "And my hand is *killing* me. I could use a painkiller or two."

Deputy Sparks grinned and inclined his head toward the cell. "Well, quiet except for that."

"All this bellyaching is making me hungry. I'm off to see what I can find."

Needles took off for the break room while Alex strolled over to where Beau sat on the cot.

"You hit an officer of the law," Alex said. "You could go away for a long time."

"I wasn't aiming for you," Beau snapped.

Alex snorted. "You aren't helping your case."

"Fine. I'm sorry. Is that what you want?"

"What I want is for you to leave Annaleigh and Charlotte's boyfriend alone. Do I make myself clear? Because if I have to arrest you again, you'll be sitting in this jail cell for a very long time. Understand?"

"Yeah, I hear ya."

Deputy Sparks tossed Alex a keyring, and Alex caught it one-handed. Unlocking the cell, Alex swung the door open and motioned for Beau to exit.

"I'm not kidding, Broombotten. No more trouble from you."

Beau didn't acknowledge Alex…he just strode out of the office, slamming the door behind him.

"That went well," Deputy Sparks mused.

Alex chuckled. "I get the feeling we'll be seeing Mr. Broombotten again real soon."

"A lot sooner than you might think," Deputy Sparks said.

"What do you mean?" I asked.

"Yeah, whaddya mean?" Needles demanded as he flew into the room and landed on my shoulder, paws stuffed with pretzel sticks.

Deputy Sparks chuckled. "He walked out without his keys, wallet, and phone. He's not gonna get far."

Alex and I both laughed.

"Need my help tonight?" Deputy Sparks asked.

Alex shook his head. "No. We have this handled." He looked at his watch. "What do you have? Two hours left on your shift?"

Deputy Sparks nodded. "Sounds about right."

"Normally, I'd have you patrol the west side of the island before you clock out, but I may need you at some point tonight. Do you mind just sticking around the station?"

The sheriff's door opened, and Beau stomped back inside. "Where the hell are my keys?"

"Try looking where the sun don't shine." Needles somersaulted in the air, his wings glowing green and yellow.

Deputy Sparks slowly opened the top drawer of his desk and tossed Beau his items one at a time. "Stay out of trouble."

Once again, Beau said nothing, just turned on his heel and strode out of the office.

Deputy Sparks shook his head and smiled. "Yep, I expect we'll see him again shortly before the night is over."

I hurried over to the window and looked down. Beau texted someone, shoved the phone into his pocket, then got behind the wheel of his car.

"He's leaving," I said. "We better move."

By the time we exited the building, Beau was gone. Climbing into my Bronco, I closed my eyes, placed my hands on the steering wheel, and whispered a locator spell. Within seconds, I had Beau's location.

"You're not gonna believe where he is," I said, starting my engine.

"Where?"

"Just a couple streets over at Boos & Brews." I pulled out onto the street. "Why is he going back to the scene of the crime?"

"Don't they always?" Needles mused.

19

I pulled into the side parking lot of Boos & Brews and parked two vehicles down from Beau's car. The lot was fairly empty, which wasn't surprising, considering it was a Sunday night.

"Guess we just settle in," Alex said.

"Or we could go inside," I suggested.

Alex frowned. "He'd make us out immediately, Shayla."

I waggled my eyebrows. "Not necessarily."

Alex smiled and slowly shook his head. "Why do I get the feeling you're going to suggest something crazy?"

I grinned back at him. "He wouldn't recognize us if I glamoured us."

"Glamoured? As in, you want to make me look like someone else?"

"Something like that." I patted his hand. "Don't worry. It won't hurt."

"Haha. I'm more worried about how you're gonna make me look."

Needles flew up and perched on my headrest. *"Afraid you won't have the legs to pull off a miniskirt, Gargoyle?"*

"Very funny," Alex said.

I laughed and shook my head. "Don't worry, I'm not going to put you in a skirt and heels. But I *can* make it so we don't look like us. We could go inside, see what he's up to, and then slip out."

"I don't know…"

Needles made chicken noises. *"Is the big bad gargoyle scared?"*

"Unless you want to be bald," Alex said, "I'd suggest you stop right now, Porcupine."

Needles did a flip off my headrest and zipped back to his seat. *"I got plenty of pretzels back here to keep me happy. You two lovebirds go on inside and have a little fun."*

"Well?" I mused.

Alex sighed. "Let's do this before I change my mind."

Grinning, I centered myself and whispered a glamour spell for him. His short, dark hair became blond and shaggy, while his eyes changed shape and color. I made his square jaw more round and gave him freckles.

Alex pulled down the visor and groaned. "I look like a surfer."

Laughing, I whispered a glamour spell for myself, shook out my hair, then looked in the rear-view mirror. My auburn hair was now black and curly, and my eyes were a vivid blue. My face was also rounder, with a dimple in my left cheek.

"Well?" I asked.

"This brings role-playing to a whole new level," Alex deadpanned.

I laughed and slapped his arm. "Don't be getting any ideas."

"C'mon, let's go see if this crazy idea will work."

"Don't order drinks," Needles said from the back, his wings glowing green with merriment. *"You might get carded and then arrested for impersonating an officer."*

Alex was still grumbling as he opened the door to Boos & Brews. Three customers were sitting at the counter drinking and talking with the bartender when Alex and I entered. Everyone else was scattered about in booths. It didn't take me long to find Beau.

"I can't see who he's talking to," I said." We'll have to walk by their booth."

Alex slipped his hand into mine, and together we strolled casually across the bar and over to where Beau sat. As we passed by his booth, I glanced down to see who his companion was.

No surprise…it was Ellen Vampton.

Alex and I slid into the booth behind them, both of us in the same seat so we could overhear their conversation. We'd barely gotten situated when a server came by to take our order.

"I'll have an iced tea," I said.

"Make that two."

When she scurried away, we settled back into our vinyl seat and listened.

"I think the sheriff and that nosy game warden are on to us," Beau said.

"They have no proof of anything," Ellen said. "It'll be fine."

"You weren't the one stuck in a jail cell all day," Beau snapped.

"That was on you," Ellen said. "You and your hot head. Now, we are both in this together, so let's just make the most of it."

"I'm just not sure it's a good idea right now," Beau said. "We need to lay low for a while."

"Don't even think of backing out on me now," Ellen hissed.

"I'm not backing out," Beau said. "I just don't know how smart it is for us to—"

"Stop worrying," Ellen interrupted. "We'll meet back up in thirty minutes. We can't be seen together." There was a rustling sound as someone stood up from the booth. "Thirty minutes, Beau. Don't be late."

Our server set the drinks in front of us and asked if we needed anything else. We both shook our heads no, and she stepped over to Beau and Ellen's booth.

"Did your friend leave?" the server asked.

"Yeah," Beau said. "You can take our drinks. I just need the check."

I heard paper being torn from a pad, a brief pause, and then the movements of someone standing. When a good minute had passed with no other sound, Alex peeked his head around our booth.

"All clear. Looks like they're gone." He stood and dropped a handful of bills onto the table. "If I had to guess, I'd say they're going back to Charming Baubles."

"Do you think they worked together to kill Charlotte?"

"I'm leaning that way." He helped me up from the table. "We definitely have enough to pick them up and bring them in for formal questioning."

20

"I *still think you should have left the glamour on, Gargoyle,"* Needles said. *"Surfer boy suits you."*

We'd been parked across the street from Charming Baubles for about five minutes, but there was still no sign of Beau or Ellen. The thirty minutes was about up, so I knew we wouldn't have much longer to wait.

My pulse spiked when a car turned onto the street and headed our way. But when it parked in front of Enchanted Appliances Plus, and the driver exited the car…I frowned. "I know it's kind of dark out here, but isn't that Annaleigh's vehicle?"

Alex leaned over me and nodded. "I think so. She told us she had a meeting with Grey tonight, remember?"

"That's right. I forgot."

Annaleigh looked around, clutched her purse to her chest, then walked to the store's front door. Yanking it open, she hurried inside the dimly lit shop.

When a few more minutes passed and still no Ellen or Beau, I glanced at my watch again. "I usually have more patience than this, but I really wish these two would hurry up."

"Me too. I'm almost out of pretzels."

The banging of a door startled me, and I glanced over at Enchanted Appliances Plus. Annaleigh was hunched over and running to her car. She opened the door, threw her purse inside, then slid behind the wheel. Seconds later, tires squealing, she made a U-turn from the curb and rocketed past us. I caught a glimpse of her pale face from the streetlight overhead.

"Anyone but me got a bad feeling about that?" I mused.

Alex and I both opened our doors to exit the Bronco.

"Wait for me!" Needles exclaimed as he flew out from the back.

Alex and I jogged across the street to Grey's store. Plastering my forehead to the window, I tried to see inside, but there was only one light on in the back, so I couldn't make anything out.

Alex opened the front door with his left hand, his right hand on his service revolver. "I'll go left, you sweep right."

The minute I stepped inside, I swiveled right and scanned the store. Needles hovered near my shoulder, his wings throwing off brilliant colors.

"Dial it down a little," I hissed. "You have too much light coming from you."

Needles' wings turned a dull gray. "Better?"

"Much," I whispered.

My side of the store was crammed with ovens and dishwashers. Skirting around them, I made sure no one else was in the store and hiding…or that Grey wasn't lying dead on the floor.

"You want me to fly to the back and see what I can find?"

"Grey, this is Sheriff Stone," Alex called out as he moved toward the center aisle of the store. "Are you in here?"

I motioned for Needles to go to the back and check it out, while I moved closer to the middle aisle near Alex.

Seconds later, Needles zipped back to where we stood, his wings glowing red and blue. "Grey's here all right, but he won't be answering you."

My heart lurched. I knew what we'd find at the back of the store. I hadn't known Grey well, but he was always friendly when I came into the store, and he always waved when I saw him in town. He didn't deserve to die like this.

Alex and I hurried to where Grey had his office. The light was on inside, and when Alex and I stepped inside, I couldn't help the strangled cry.

Grey Wolfstein lay sprawled on his back, his eyes wide open…but unseeing.

I knelt down next to the body and inhaled. "Magic. Probably another death spell."

I heard a car door slam in the back alley, and my eyes met Alex's. "Want me and Needles to check it out?"

Alex nodded. "Go ahead. I'll call this in and get Deputy Sparks and Doc out here."

I stood and motioned for Needles to follow me. When I reached the back door, I slowly eased it open and peered through the crack. No surprise, Ellen and Beau were at the back door of Charming Baubles.

"How hard can this be?" Ellen demanded. "I thought you said you could get it open! I need those charmed pieces Charlotte was supposed to sell me. I *know* this time they'll work."

"I can get it open," Beau hissed. "It will just take a while. Wards were never Charlotte's strong suit."

Needles zipped past me—wings fluttering so quickly they sounded like a storm of angry bees—and yanked two quills from his back. *"Step back from that door or suffer the consequences!"*

Ellen screamed and swatted at Needles, but he was too fast for her. Sticking both quills under her chin, he backed her up against the brick building.

"My turn."

I hurled a bolt of magic at Beau, but not before he got a shot in as well. Pain sliced through my body, and I looked down, surprised at the blood pouring from my side.

"Gotcha!" Beau exclaimed. "Bet you weren't expecting that."

Needles cried out in anger, lifted both quills in the air, and stabbed Beau through the neck.

"What the—"

"Bet you weren't expecting that!" Needles yanked out two more quills and stabbed him again, this time in the face.

Beau howled and staggered backward, looking like a human pincushion. It wasn't the first time Needles had used that move.

Smiling, I raised my hand and sent another bolt of magic streaming through Beau's chest. His body shook and his eyes rolled in his head. He hit the ground hard and didn't stand back up.

"He made me come here," Ellen said. "I didn't want to, but he—"

"Save it. We know the truth. We heard the two of you talking in your booth at Boos & Brews tonight."

Ellen scowled, her eyes flashing with anger. "All Charlotte had to do was sell me the jewelry. But no, she had to have a conscience. That jewelry belongs to me!"

"So that's what this is about? You were trying to break in to get more charmed jewelry?"

"Something in that store will work for me! I just know it!"

Disgusted, I whipped her around to face the building, ignoring the throbbing in my side. Conjuring up a pair of handcuffs, I slapped them over her wrists.

I heard sirens in the distance and knew Deputy Sparks and Doc were on their way.

"Everything all right out here?" Alex asked.

"Princess Shayla has been hit." Needles stood on Beau's chest, his wings glowing bright red, and a fierce snarl on his face.

"I'm okay," I said. "And they both just admitted to trying to break in to Charlotte's store to steal some jewelry."

"I don't care about the jewelry," Alex said, running his hands lightly over me. "Where were you hit?"

I held up my hand and backed away. "You know I have the ability to heal quickly. It's just a flesh wound. We need to talk about the fact they weren't here at the time of Grey's death, so that only leaves one other person."

Alex crossed his arms over his chest and scowled at me. "And I suppose next you'll tell me you want to go with me? Even though you're injured?"

Needles flew to my shoulder. *"If the princess says she's up to it, then she's up to it, Gargoyle. Let's go get Annaleigh."*

21

Euthelva Hexly's home was pitch black when Alex pulled my Bronco to a stop in front of her mailbox. Euthelva's and Annaleigh's cars were parked in the driveway, so I figured they had to be around somewhere.

Deputy Sparks had hauled Ellen and Beau away while Doc and Finn processed the scene at Enchanted Appliances Plus. Assuring us they could handle it, Alex, Needles, and I sped off to arrest Annaleigh.

Fingering the yucca poultice I'd quickly conjured up on the ride over to apply to my bleeding side, I carefully exited my vehicle, Needles right behind me.

"You doing okay, Princess?" Needles asked.

"I think the bleeding has already stopped."

Euthelva's front door was locked, so Alex, Needles, and I tiptoed around back and down to Annaleigh's cottage, where every light in the house was blazing.

"I still can't believe Annaleigh killed Charlotte," I said. "Her own cousin. And why? Because she was going to sell the building? Absolutely senseless."

"We know James is probably inside the cottage," Alex said. "We need to make sure we have him out of the way, and he doesn't get hurt."

"Unless James is also involved," Needles said. *"At this point, nothing would surprise me."*

I gasped. "You mean like Annaleigh and James had this planned all along?"

Needles dropped onto my shoulder. *"Maybe."*

"How do you want to do this?" I asked Alex. "We all go in the front? Or do you want to go around back and see if there's another way inside?"

"I'll take the back. You and Needles see what you can discover out here. Don't go in until I give the sign. Got it?"

"Got it," I said.

Alex jogged around the back while I crept slowly to the front window. I peered inside, Needles still sitting on my shoulder.

"Whaddya see, Princess?"

"James is tied to a chair, and it looks like he's bleeding from the head or temple. Annaleigh is pacing near him, and I'd say she's yelling from the look on her face."

"Looks like this James guy really wasn't involved, after all."

I heard a faint rustling behind me and turned. Alex put his finger to his lips and motioned me over to him. Needles flew off my shoulder and stayed near the window.

"There's no back door," Alex whispered. "Only one way in and out from what I can see. There are two screened windows opened in the back, but that's it."

"James is tied to a chair, and Annaleigh looks like she's about to have a breakdown inside. She's pacing and yelling."

"Any sign of Euthelva?" Alex asked.

I shook my head. "I didn't see her."

"I don't like that. I want to know where Euthelva is."

"Do you think she's involved as well?" I asked.

Alex shrugged. "I honestly don't know. But I hate surprises."

"Well," Needles said as he hovered near the window, still looking inside, *"then you're gonna hate this next part."*

Alex and I rushed toward the window, but before we could reach it, the front door opened and Euthelva stood in the doorway.

"Come inside. If you make any sudden moves, I swear, I'll kill James."

I slid my gaze to Alex, but he simply nodded. "Understood. Shayla and I don't want anyone else hurt."

"I'm afraid that won't be possible," Euthelva said. "All of you in here. Now."

Alex and I stepped inside the cottage, and I got my first good look at what was going on. James was, indeed, tied to a chair, but he seemed coherent. At least, he was able to focus on Alex and me when we entered the cottage. Annaleigh, her face pale and frightened, stood next to an end table.

"Where's the porcupine that's always with you?" Euthelva snapped. "I know he's around here somewhere."

Had Needles flown off somewhere? I hadn't even given him another thought when Euthelva ordered us inside.

"He stayed behind at Enchanted Appliances Plus." I narrowed my eyes at Euthelva. "I'm sure you know why."

Euthelva slammed the door shut. "None of this would have been necessary if Charlotte hadn't lost her mind and sold the building!"

Annaleigh whimpered. "I just don't understand how you could have killed Charlotte and Mr. Wolfstein. Why, Momma?"

"Why?" Euthelva bellowed. "Why? I'll tell you why, dear daughter. Because you are a *Normal*. You can't do magic."

Annaleigh winced as though her mother had just slapped her. "I'm aware. But you always said that didn't matter."

Euthelva laughed bitterly. "Of course it didn't matter *then*. You had a great job and were making lots of money. But Charlotte ruined all that by not only leaving the island and taking that profit with her, but then she went and sold the building! How would we live without that income?" Sparks flew from Euthelva's fingertips. "How could she be so *selfish*? Thinking only of herself? Didn't I take in that ungrateful brat when her parents died? Did I have to? No. But I did because she was my sister's kid. And how does she repay me? By yanking the rug out from under me. Without an income, we'll lose everything!"

Tears spilled down Annaleigh's cheeks. "I could have gotten another job, Momma. I do have skills, you know. I could have continued making jewelry and selling it on the regular Internet. Humans on the mainland would buy it, I'm sure. You didn't even give me a chance."

Euthelva scoffed. "We need actual *money* to live, you fool. I'm too old to just scrape by."

"And so by killing Charlotte," I said, "you knew Annaleigh would inherit the business and the building."

"My plan was to talk Annaleigh into selling the building, but at a much higher price than what Charlotte was selling it for." Euthelva scoffed. "She was all but giving it away to that man. And he wasn't even family!"

"So what?" I mused. "You waited until Charlotte was outside in the back parking lot, ran out, and killed her?"

"Don't be crass," Euthelva snapped. "I waited until she went outside to call Brooms Away, asked her for help, then as we walked toward my car, I confronted her about selling the building." Euthelva snorted. "She had the *audacity* to tell me Annaleigh was okay with her decision, so I really didn't have a say." She smiled menacingly. "So I made sure she would never have a say in anything ever again too. Crushed her throat in a matter of seconds, then tossed her behind the dumpster like the trash she was." She let out a bark of laughter. "On my next trip out with a box, when I saw Beau in the parking lot by the fence, I was terrified he'd discover the body behind the dumpster. But he didn't."

Movement caught my eye, and I saw Needles hovering near the doorway behind Euthelva.

"I loved her," James whispered. "She was kind and gentle, and you killed her simply because you were afraid your own daughter couldn't support you in the life you'd grown accustomed to? Do you know how shallow that sounds?"

Screaming, Euthelva sent a wave of magic so powerful, it lifted James bodily in the air and sent him crashing into the wall three feet behind him. The chair splintered, and James fell to the floor.

I turned to give her my own jolt of magic, but Euthelva was prepared. Lifting one hand to me, and the other to Alex, she blasted us both at the same time. Alex shifted into his gargoyle form, so when the blast hit him, it only caused him to stumble backward. I whispered the word I used to erect an invisibility shield, and with no time to spare, the shield went up as the magic pulsed my way.

Unfortunately, Annaleigh had no idea I was going to erect an invisibility shield, and in an effort to save me, she jumped in front of her mother's stream—the magic hitting her in the chest. Annaleigh screamed as the magic and electricity coursed through her body.

"No!" Euthelva shouted, dropping her hands to her side. "You fool, Annaleigh! Why would you do that?"

"Because she's not heartless like you!" Needles hissed, rapidly throwing quills at Euthelva, one after the other, distracting her as Alex shifted back to his human form and threw his Binder, encasing Euthelva in a huge magic-free bubble.

I dropped to my knees, checking to see if Annaleigh had a pulse. When I didn't feel one, I panicked. My magic could heal plants and animals. I had no idea if I could heal another supernatural.

"Is she breathing?" James asked as he crawled over to us.

I shook my head. "No."

"Let me. My gift is healing. I usually do it through jewelry, but I can do it without."

He laid his hands over Annaleigh's chest and whispered a spell I vaguely knew. Seconds later, Annaleigh's eyes flew open, and she sat up, gasping for air.

"You okay?" I asked.

Annaleigh shook her head, tears rolling down her cheeks. "No, I'm not okay. Not only have I lost my best friend and cousin, but my *mother* killed her and almost killed me. I'll *never* be okay."

James gathered Annaleigh into his arms. "Yes, you will. It will just take time."

As Annaleigh continued to sob against James, I stood and hurried over to Alex and Needles.

"You were right, Needles," I said as I glared at Euthelva inside the bubble. "We weren't going to like what happened next."

"How'd you get into the house?" Alex asked.

"I used a quill and cut through one of the screens. Flew right in. Figured you two had it under control, and all I needed to do

was wait until I was needed." He settled down onto my shoulder. *"Can't believe Euthelva killed her own niece over money."*

"And because she didn't want to work a job," I said. "She'd rather rely on her daughter, and when she thought *that* wouldn't work out, she killed another man."

"It wasn't fair I was cursed with a Normal daughter!" Euthelva raged from inside her bubble. "Her father and I could both do magic! She should have been able to, as well!"

"Get her out of here," I growled, pissed Euthelva would say something so callous in front of Annaleigh, who was still crying in James' arms. "I'm sick of her nasty hatred."

The truth was, I was sick of all the prejudice against the Normals. It wasn't fair, and it wasn't their fault. I needed to speak to Dad and GiGi and see what could be done to educate other supernaturals on the island.

Alex withdrew his cell phone out of his pocket. "Want me to call Zane or PADA?"

"Call Zane and see if he and Kara are free to come get her," I said. "If they are, Zane can call PADA and tell them he and Kara can take the run."

22

Three days later, I was sitting with my back against Dad's trunk and filling him in on everything that had happened with Euthelva. As it turned out, Zane and Kara were in between assignments, so they flew to Enchanted Island the next morning to pick up Euthelva and escort her to PADA's prison where she would be stripped of all her magic and incarcerated for the rest of her life.

"And all this death because of money," Dad said. *"I know I have lived thousands of years, but I still cannot understand how supernaturals can kill each other over such trivial things as money."*

"Money and jealousy, Dad. That's how a lot of our cases end up."

Dad sighed. *"That is unfortunate."*

"But there was some good that came from it," I said. "James asked Annaleigh to move to Hollow Springs and help out in his store. Strictly professional, of course. It seems they bonded over their shared sorrow. Annaleigh will continue to make jewelry, and she won't have to stay on the island where there are reminders of her pain. When I went to visit her yesterday, she'd just come from finalizing the sale of Charlotte's building to Grey's son. He wants to honor his father's memory by continuing with the expansion."

"I am delighted there is good from all this sorrow," Dad said.

I smiled as Needles drifted down from Dad's branches and landed on my shoulder, his wings shimmering gold and silver.

"How is your side healing?" Dad asked.

"All better. Which is no surprise." I laughed. "If I can be shot in the shoulder and feel almost perfect two days later, trust me, a slice to my ribs isn't going to keep me down."

"I suppose not," Dad said.

"Both Ellen and Beau have been brought up on charges," I said. "Since it's Ellen's first big offense, though, she'll probably get off lighter than Beau."

"Let us talk of happier things. How is Serena feeling?"

"Second trimester is going smoothly. More cravings and mood swings, but she's handling it like a pro."

Dad chuckled. *"Good. And the wedding plans?"*

"On track. I'm going to use Diana Hedge, a local witch who owns Magical Stitches, a sewing shop in town. Serena used her for her wedding veil, and I know she could use the job."

"Diana Hedge? Is that the young girl whose roommate was killed a while back?"

"That's her. She stayed on the island after all that happened, and her shop is doing okay, but I know she could use all the help she can get. So I figured, why go off the island for a wedding dress? Why not have it made locally?"

One of Dad's branches lowered, and a leaf brushed my cheek. *"You have a kind heart, Shayla. It is important to not only care for the nature and animals on Enchanted Island, but to also care for the supernaturals and non-supernaturals who live here as well. For they, too, are part of the island."*

I smiled and leaned back against Dad's trunk. "Spoken like a true Genius Loci."

Dad chuckled. *"Perhaps."*

"I also have Iris working on the flowers, and Serena, Tamara, and Zoie are all working on the design of the cake. Not sure why it takes the three of them, but it does."

"Have you told GiGi she is to be the flower girl?" Dad asked.

Needles did a somersault off my shoulder, his wings glowing purple. *"You mean you didn't hear her squeal of excitement all the way out here in Black Forest?"*

"I did not," Dad said. *"I take it she was happy with that assignment?"*

"Very," I said.

"Good. I wanted to speak to you about another matter if you have some time, Shayla?"

"Of course." I sat up straight and turned to face his trunk. "What's up?"

"I received word earlier this morning from Alfisol—through one of the woodland creatures—that someone was on the north side of the island yesterday."

I gasped. "What? Seriously? Who would dare?" I frowned. "Wait. Who's Alfisol?"

"Alfisol is just the name I gave him when he fled to the island for sanctuary some thousand or so years ago."

"Alfisol?" I mused. "That's a forestry term, right?"

"It is."

I furrowed my brow in concentration, trying to recall what it meant. "Alfisol is a fertile soil that forms under the forest and where clay accumulates."

"Right again, Daughter of my Heart."

"And he's a supernatural?" I mused. "I guess so if he fled here—wait, did you say a *thousand* years ago?"

"Give or take a few hundred years," Dad said. *"Anyway, he is understandably concerned with this recent trespassing on the north side. As am I."*

I knew a few creatures lived on the north side of the island. Kraken liked both the north and west, but Randor preferred to stay solely on the north side. Randor wasn't a dragon shifter but an actual *dragon* who was also over a thousand years old.

"What kind of supernatural is this Alfisol guy? And why is he living on the north side of the island?"

Needles settled back onto my shoulder. *"He likes to be called Al."*

I snorted. "Al? Okay, what kind of supernatural is Al?"

"He's a golem," Dad said.

I gasped. "What? A golem? Like, a *golem, golem*? One of those scary creatures formed from clay who hurts people?"

Dad tsked. *"Shayla, you know better than to judge a supernatural simply on what you hear from rumors. Do not be like others who are so quick to judge."*

I winced. "You're right. I'm sorry. I'm sure this Al guy is…" I wasn't sure what word I was looking for to describe a golem. "I'm sure he's a nice guy."

"Lame," Needles snickered. *"But you'd be right. Al keeps to himself even more than Randor the dragon. Heck, even Kraken is seen more often than Al."*

"I'd say. I've never heard of this Al guy or even heard of the fact we have a *golem* living on the island. Do Mom and GiGi know?"

"I believe so," Dad said.

"Wow. A golem on Enchanted Island."

"Yes, and he is concerned about recent activity near his home. I would appreciate it if you could find time to speak with him, and then see if you can track down who would dare disobey my one and only rule to living on Enchanted Island."

"I'll get right on it," I promised. "Needles, wanna go talk to a golem?"

Needles hovered near my face, his wings glowing green with excitement. *"I'd love nothing more, Princess."*

* * *

Are you ready for the next book in the series? Then click here and get Deadly Feud and find out what happens when a well-liked vampire dentist and his wife are kidnapped on Enchanted Island. My Book

* * *

Love the idea of a Valkyrie witch teaming up with a Fallen Angel to solve crimes? Then the paranormal cozy series, A Kara Hilder Mystery, should be right up your alley! This crime-solving duo not only works for their supernatural town of Mystic Cove, but they also work for the Paranormal Apprehension and Detention Agency—which means they travel a lot to take down bad guys. Find out what happens when a Valkyrie with magical abilities teams up with a Fallen Angel in Book 1, Sounds of Murder My Book

Have you read the hilarious adventures of Ryli Sinclair and Aunt Shirley? This traditional cozy mystery series is always fast-paced and laugh-out-loud funny. But what else would you expect from Aunt Shirley—a woman who has at least two deadly weapons on her at all times and carries her tequila in a flask shoved down her shirt? Book 1 is Picture Perfect Murder! My Book

Love the idea of a bookstore/bar set in the picturesque wine country of Sonoma County? Then join Jaycee, Jax, Gramps, Tillie, and the whole gang in this traditional cozy series as they solve murders while slinging suds and chasing bad guys in this family-oriented series. My Book

Do you love the idea of a time-traveling, cold-case solving witch? Then Lexi and her side-kick detective familiar, Rex the Rat, are just what you're looking for! Check out their first stop to 1988 in Time After Time My Book

How about a seaside mystery? My stepdaughter and I write a mystery where high school seniors pair up with their grandma and great-aunt! Book one, Seaside & Homicide: My Book

Or maybe you're in the mood for a romantic comedy…heavy on comedy and light on sweet romance? Then the Trinity Falls series is for you! My Book

Looking for a paranormal cozy series about a midlife witch looking to make a new start with a new career? Then A Witch in the Woods is the book series for you! A game warden witch, a talking/flying porcupine, and a gargoyle sheriff! My Book

ABOUT THE AUTHOR

Jenna writes in the genres of cozy/paranormal cozy/ romantic comedy. Her humorous characters and stories revolve around over-the-top family members, creative murders, and there's always a positive element of the military in her stories. Jenna currently lives in Missouri with her fiancé, step-daughter, Nova Scotia duck tolling retriever dog, Brownie, and her tuxedo-cat, Whiskey. She is a former court reporter turned educator turned full-time writer. She has a Master's degree in Special Education, and an Education Specialist degree in Curriculum and Instruction. She also spent twelve years in full-time ministry.

When she's not writing, Jenna likes to attend beer and wine tastings, go antiquing, visit craft festivals, and spend time with her family and friends. Check out her website at http://www.jennastjames.com/. Don't forget to sign up for the newsletter so you can keep up with the latest releases! You can also friend request her on Facebook at jennastjamesauthor/ or catch her on Instagram at authorjennastjames.

www.ingramcontent.com/pod-product-compliance
Lightning Source LLC
Chambersburg PA
CBHW071127151224
19024CB00030B/572

9 798354 832255

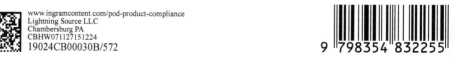